THE WONDERS OF THE PECULIAR PARASOL

A DRAGONSTONE STORY, BOOK I

BY
MARK M. EVEN

With contributions and inspiration from
Gina L. Even

Illustrations by Anna Canfield

CRESTINGWAVE
PUBLISHING

THE WONDERS OF THE PECULIAR PARASOL
A Dragonstone Story, Book I

Written by Mark M. Even

Copyright © 2021 by Even Books, LLP

ISBN: 978-0-9889048-2-8

Additional material and story editing by Kris Neely
Copy editing by Christine LePorte
Layout by Lazar Kackarovski
Cover Art and Chapter Illustrations by Lan Nguyen

Dedicated to all the Even children and grandchildren.

Thank you to our reviewers:
Amanda
Dick & Pat
Troon
The Licata's

Special thanks to Carter for giving us a much-needed perspective and to Nora, Henry, Helena, Penelope, and Camilla Stewart for their wonderful imaginations

And to Mrs. E and her reading class.
To Mary G for her help.
To Joe and Joyce for their love and support.
Many thanks to Dana and Laura at Cresting Wave Publishing.

DESCENDANTS OF PHEF
– FAMILY TREE

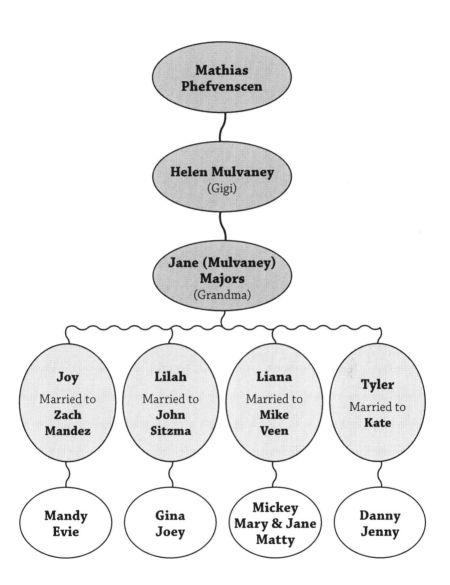

TABLE OF CONTENTS

CHAPTER 1

THE PARASOL

ANDY MANDEZ SAT IN the back seat of the car, looking at the monotonous cornfields lining the highway. "Mom, how much longer to Grandma's house?" she whined.

"Amanda Jane Mandez! Have a little patience, will you?" her mother scolded. "We've only been on the road for fifteen minutes. Really, sometimes I think you act like a five-year-old!"

Mandy huffed and looked over at the small gift bag on which the big green Hulk was saying, 'Happy Birthday, Human!' Her cousin Mickey Veen had turned ten years old last week on July fourth, and he was going to be at Grandma's today, too. Then she frowned because she knew Mickey got a cell phone for his birthday. The bag held a gift card for the iTunes store so he could buy some apps for his phone.

"Mom, why can't I have a cell phone? Mickey has one now, and he just turned ten. I was ten in February—why can't I have one if he already has one?"

"We've talked about this, Mandy. You promised you would get your grades up, and then you didn't deliver. So—no grades, no phone. If you do better in the first semester this fall, we will get you a phone for Christmas. Now, settle down. I can see Grandma's town up ahead, so we will be there in a few minutes, and then you get to spend all day with Gina, Mickey, and Grandma."

Mandy looked ahead through the windshield and saw two church steeples peeking above the trees. The steeples always alerted her that they were close to Grandma's house. She smiled after being reminded that one of her other cousins, Gina, was going to be there, too. Mom and her twin sisters were going on a shopping trip to the big city. They'd decided it would be fun if they brought their oldest kids to Grandma's house where they planned to meet up for breakfast. Then they would leave the kids with Grandma for the day while they went shopping. Gina was Mandy's favorite cousin, even though she could be a little bossy. Mickey, well, he was just Mickey. Gina and Mandy tolerated his antics when they were all together.

Mandy unbuckled her seatbelt as soon as her mom pulled into Grandma's driveway.

"Don't forget Mickey's present!" her mom shouted after Mandy had already hopped out of the car.

"I have it, Mom!" Mandy retorted. "You don't always have to remind me, you know!" She ran past her aunts' cars and in the front door. "Hi, Grandma!" she said as she gave her grandmother a big hug. "Hi, Aunt Lilah. Hi, Aunt Laina!" Then she thrust the gift bag to Mickey, who was beaming the second he saw her carry it into the house. "Here—happy birthday, Mickey."

"Another iTunes gift card! Oh boy, now I can get even more games for my phone!" Mickey shouted, holding the card up for all to see.

"That's what we gave him, too," Gina said to Mandy as she put her arm around Mandy's shoulders. "Grandma made her famous cinnamon rolls for breakfast but said we couldn't have any until you guys got here. Let's grab some before Mickey touches them all."

As usual, at every house where Gina slept even one night or stayed one day, the table held books. Lots of them. Two books here, three books there—it was always like that because Gina was always reading. *For her age,* Mandy thought, *she talks like a college kid sometimes!*

Mandy, Gina, and Mickey sat around the kitchen table eating their cinnamon rolls and drinking orange juice while their moms joined Grandma in the dining room to eat and chat. After the kids had spent about a half-hour watching Mickey select new iPhone games and taking turns playing them, their moms bustled into the kitchen with dishes. The moms said quick goodbyes and hurried out the door for their shopping trip.

Grandma asked the kids to help clean up and then said, "I called your great-grandmother and told her we'd come to visit today. Let's get in the car and go now."

The children loved their great-grandma, whom they called Gigi. Gina quickly shouted, "I get the window," and ran to the car to get the best spot in the back seat. Mandy reluctantly let Mickey get the other window. That meant she got stuck in the middle, but at least she could sit by Gina. Grandma started her old brown Pontiac Bonneville and headed off to Gigi's house in Grandma's hometown of Remsen, twenty minutes away.

The girls chatted with Grandma during the drive, while Mickey ignored them and played a video game on his cell phone. When they arrived at Gigi's, she was sitting on the front porch of the old three-story house. The children raced up the steps and took turns giving Gigi a big hug. She led them into the house, where she had fresh chocolate chip cookies and lemonade on the kitchen table.

After snacking and chatting, the kids went off to play, leaving Grandma and Gigi in the kitchen having "grown-up" talk.

"Let's play Monopoly," Mandy offered.

"Oh, Mandy, you always want to play that. That game takes forever!" Gina grumbled. "I know, let's play hide-and-seek!"

Mandy rolled her eyes. *Once again, Gina's trying to be in charge,* she thought. They decided to do rock-paper-scissors to decide who was "it." Mandy was happy she at least won that, and Mickey got stuck being it, so the girls ran off through the big old house to hide while he counted to fifty.

Mandy ran into the dining room with the built-in cabinets that covered an entire wall. She knew there was a cupboard there that she could squeeze into, and she opened the door to hide in it. As she was shutting the door, she heard Gina's footsteps running up the stairs to the second floor.

Mickey shouted, "Ready or not, here I come!" Rushing to the dining room, he opened the cupboard door. "Found you, Mandy. You hid in there the last time we played."

Then he stopped and listened. Mandy heard a loud squeak coming from above and then chased after Mickey as he bolted up the stairs. Instead of staying on the next level, Mickey ran to a narrow set of steps that led to the attic. He turned and whispered to Mandy, "She's up here. That creaky door to the attic made that noise."

Mandy followed Mickey into the attic, and when the door squeaked loudly, there was a loud crash just ahead of them.

Lying on the floor was a wooden coat rack with old winter coats, and Gina's feet sticking out of the mess.

"Found you, Gina! Now one of you is it!" Mickey cried triumphantly.

Gina struggled to get out from under the mess, giggling. "I heard you come in and tried to make sure I was hidden, and then tripped on this old coat rack."

Mandy looked down and saw something peculiar on the floor amongst the coats. It was like an umbrella, but different. The handle was wooden, carved to look like a dragon with its tail curved at the bottom. The umbrella's fabric was a faded beige, decorated with branches or vines with different-colored flower buds coming off them. At the very top was a dull white knob. Was it glass, or was it a crystal? Mandy picked the umbrella up and wiped dust off the knob to see it better. It looked more like a crystal—a polished stone, she decided.

She said, "Hey, look at this dirty old thing. It sure doesn't look like it would keep anyone dry. See how flimsy it is? Water would probably soak right through it."

"Let me see!" said Gina as she grabbed it from Mandy. "Let's go ask Gigi about it. I think it's kind of pretty, but weird." As she walked across the dimly lit attic, she passed through a beam of sunlight shining through the window. Suddenly, the room flashed with a bright red light.

"Wow—what was that?" said Mickey. "It looks like it came from the glass knob!"

Mandy stared thoughtfully at the crystal stone. She had seen it turn red, and now its color was quickly fading. She looked at her cousins, who stared back at her, unsure of what to say or do.

"Gigi!" Mandy yelled, and the kids all turned and sprinted across the dusty attic, through the doorway and, without closing the door, descended the narrow dark stairs as quickly as they could without falling.

They ran into the kitchen and stopped with a lurch in front of Gigi. Gigi looked at the umbrella in Gina's hands, put her own hands to her face, and said, "Oh my! The... the parasol!"

Grandma looked at her grandchildren, then at Gigi, and said softly but sternly, "Mom, I thought you threw that thing away."

Mickey asked, "What's a parasol?"

Gigi said, "Oh, it's a special type of umbrella used to block the sun and give shade. That one is not waterproof, though, so you don't want to use it on a rainy day. This parasol has been in my family for many years. I used to walk around town with it resting open on my shoulder and twirl it around like a princess." Gigi smiled, sweetly, at her memories.

"Now, don't you start putting stories in their head as you did to me," said Grandma.

Gigi closed her eyes, took a breath, and said, "You're right, Jane. That must all be behind me. So—why don't you kids go outside and play so we can talk, OK?"

Mandy looked at her cousins. Gina grabbed her by the hand, and they both turned toward the back door. Gigi shooed them away.

In the backyard, the kids moved to stand under the spreading branches of an old apple tree, its leaves green and its multiple branches heavy with fruits.

Mandy said, "I suppose we should have told her about the red flash. And—didn't Grandma seem kind of upset about seeing the parasol?"

Mickey said, "Yeah, I guess. I don't know. Let's... let's walk over to the park and play on the swings." He headed off with Gina trailing behind him, carrying the parasol.

Mandy was left alone in the dappled shade of the tree. She sighed and started after them. As she walked, Mandy watched Gina open the parasol and rest it on her shoulder, just like Gigi had described. She started twirling it, looking around as if a little embarrassed.

Mandy chuckled but then almost bumped into Gina, who had stopped dead in her tracks.

"Hey," Mandy said, "what'd you stop for?"

But Gina didn't move.

Mandy stepped in front of Gina to see what was wrong. She gasped at what she saw: Gina stood there, frozen. Her mouth was open as if to say something. Mandy was about to tell her cousin to stop joking around, but then she looked into Gina's dark hazel eyes. They were stone still. Not blinking at all. Like the eyes of a statue.

Mandy cried. "Mickey! Help! Help! Something is wrong with Gina!"

Mickey rushed back to them and looked at the statue that was Gina. Small beads of sweat broke out on his freckled face as he poked Gina's shoulder, waved his hands in her face, and spoke her name louder and louder. Nothing!

Hitching up his worn blue Levi's and pulling down on his dusty white T-shirt, he even tried to pick up Gina and move her. He tried a second time. And a third. Nothing; a complete bust. She wouldn't *budge*. It was like she was cemented to the gray sidewalk. He couldn't even push her over.

He moved to stand in front of Gina, looking into her face. "What's wrong with her, Mandy?" Using the back of his right hand, he quickly wiped away small tears.

Turning away from the awful scene of her cousins, Mandy felt tears well in her own eyes. She wiped them away and was turning back to Mickey when she saw something out of the corner of her eye. "Look," she stammered. "Look at the, the... stone! On top of the parasol!"

It wasn't its original dull white anymore. It was once again glowing bright red.

Mandy said, "We better get Grandma."

Just as Mandy turned to run, Gina lurched awake, snapped the parasol shut, and shouted, "Holy cow!" at the top of her lungs. She broke into a run, head down, legs pumping, and sprinted toward the house, shouting, "Gigi! Gigi! You won't believe it! *Gigi!*" as Mandy and Mickey chased after her.

CHAPTER 2

STORYWORLD

MANDY CAUGHT UP TO Gina as the two of them had to slow down suddenly to fling open the screen door in the back of the house and squeeze through it, cross the musty mudroom with its white walls, and enter the kitchen. Mickey followed close behind.

Trying desperately to catch her breath, Gina said, "Gigi, Gigi, you won't believe what happened! It was incredible!"

Mickey panted, memories painting his face. "No, wait! Wait! Listen to me—Gina was in a *trance*! A trance, for like five or ten minutes. She didn't move an inch, and we couldn't move her. We couldn't *budge* her—it was like she'd turned into a ten-ton statue! I don't know what happened to her!"

With her hands on the knees of her threadbare jeans, bent over still catching her breath, Gina gasped out a soft reply, "Wait, no, wait, wait. It's OK; I was in... Storyworld!"

At this pronouncement, Gigi smiled, the act crinkling the skin at the corners of her blue eyes. She nodded slowly as if familiar with the news.

Gigi motioned for them all to sit at the kitchen table. "Oh, I hoped this would happen! Now, calm down and catch your breath. I want to hear *all* about it."

"Where's Grandma?" Mandy asked. "Let's tell her too!"

"Oh, your grandma went to the store to get some things for your lunch," Gigi explained, glancing at the old grandfather clock, which *tick-tocked* as rhythmically as ever. "She won't be back for a little while.

"Besides," Gigi continued, "the parasol—well, it never really worked for her. I used to tell her about all the adventures I went on with it, and she would get so excited, hoping it might finally work for her. But it never did."

She continued, "You saw how upset she got when she saw the parasol, even after all this time. I think it's best we keep your Storyworld adventure our little secret for right now. OK?"

The kids looked at each other for confirmation, then nodded in unison.

"Now, Gina," said Gigi, "tell us what happened."

"Wait," Mandy interjected, remembering something her great-grandmother said. "Let's go back for a minute—you hoped this would happen?"

"Well, yes," said Gigi softly. "You see, when I was about your age, I too found the parasol—in the very same attic you did. My parents told me it was just a family heirloom. They never even hinted about... what it could do. That I discovered on my own. And the result was a list of amazing adventures."

Gigi's head slid down as she looked at her hands, her silver hair moved forward to frame her now shadowed face. "I'm not sure they ever believed all the stories I told them about those adventures. And... the parasol worked for me for about a year, and then—it just quit working. I was very frustrated and sad. And as I said, it never worked at all for your grandma. And she *never* let your mothers or your uncle play with it."

Gigi lifted her head and beamed a great smile, saying, "I'm so happy it worked for you, Gina. And now I want to hear about *your* adventure."

"So do we!" Mandy said, and Mickey nodded.

Gina sat down, and everyone gathered around her, anxiously waiting for her story to unfold.

"I was in a completely different land and time. I wasn't wearing these clothes anymore. I was wearing a beautiful red party dress. I had a big red silk bow in my hair, red ankle-length socks, and the shiniest red heels you ever saw. The parasol was on my shoulder.

"There were no cars on the broad streets, but there were horse-drawn carriages all heading towards a castle.

"I wondered out loud where in the world I was. From behind me, a man's voice said that I was in Storyworld. And he called me *Princess* Gina! I jumped. I was so startled! I turned around, and there was a man who looked like a fancy butler or something, all dressed in black and white—actually, he reminded me of a great big penguin.

"I had so many questions for him. I asked who he was, how he knew my name, what Storyworld is, how I got there... but he just cut me off with a wave of his white-gloved hand.

"He explained that he was the valet—of the parasol! And that because I now had the parasol, his job was to be my guide and protector whenever I was living a story in Storyworld, which, he told me, is the realm of the magic parasol."

"OK, whatever," Mandy interrupted. "But you haven't told us how you got to Storyworld. One second you're walking along, and then the next second you're standing right on the sidewalk, frozen solid!"

"Hang on, I'll get to that," Gina said, "but let me finish telling you what the valet told me about *how* the parasol works. To begin with, you must use the parasol on a sunny day, because it gets its power from the energy of the sun! The person holding the parasol will be 'told a story'"—here, Gina made air quotes with her fingers— "by...*living in the story as if it was real.*"

"No way," Mandy breathed.

"Yes, way" Gina said. "The valet then told me that there is *one essential rule* about the parasol. Each user is permitted only one question about the parasol itself. The user may ask questions about the story they're experiencing, but—only one question about the parasol and its magic from each user will ever be answered."

Mickey interrupted, eyes wide with wonder, "So? What did you ask?"

Gina replied, "I'll get to that. So, I knew what I wanted to ask about the parasol, but first, I wanted to know who I was talking to, so I asked his name. He said he didn't remember what his name had been because it had been eons since anyone had called him anything other than The Valet. I decided to call him J.T.—you know, short for 'Just The Valet.'

"And then I went ahead and asked him how the parasol got its magic powers."

Gigi interjected, "That's an excellent question. I wish I had thought of that one because I've always wondered."

"Thanks," Gina said proudly. "J.T. said that many, many hundreds of years ago, I had an ancestor who was a powerful wizard. J.T. was *his* squire and valet, too! The wizard's name was Mathias Phefvenscen, but people just called him 'Phef, the wizard.' He had a great-granddaughter named Blanchetta, whom he loved very much—in fact, they both loved each other very much and visited each other often.

"Whenever she visited, he would make up wonderful stories to tell her at bedtime until she fell asleep. Phef loved making up stories to tell Blanchetta. He often told J.T. it was the thing that made him happiest in the whole world—which is saying something when you're a wizard!"

Mandy and the others chuckled and nodded. Gina brushed a wisp of hair from her forehead and went on.

"But, when Phef got really old, he... he lost a good deal of the ability to speak. Although this made him feel quite sad, he was determined that stories should be a key part of Blanchetta's life. So, as a gift for her next birthday he gave her a handmade case of dark walnut, covered with red rubies, green emeralds, and white diamonds. And inside that case was an enchanted parasol. Now according to J.T., it would have been Blanchetta's tenth birthday when she got the gift."

Gina continued, "Phef placed a good spell on the parasol so it would magically tell her a story when she played with it. Sadly, shortly after Blanchetta's birthday, Phef died, and then the parasol quit working for her on her eleventh birthday.

"But, according to J.T., the magic *has remained for other generations.* Actually, for all ten-year-old children—as long as all of the other conditions are met."

"What conditions?" blurted Mandy.

Gina said, "I asked J.T. But he couldn't answer because... I'd already asked my one parasol question."

Mandy kicked at the floor with the toe of her scuffed tennis shoe. "Darn it!"

Gina said, "I know, I know. But wait, I'm not done with the whole story yet!"

Mandy crossed her arms across her chest, raised her eyebrows, and said, "Well, go on then!"

Gina smirked and said, "Before I could argue with J.T., a golden carriage came noisily up the wide street. The carriage was for some sort of high person as it was intricately carved and adorned with precious jewels in multiple colors and streamers in a variety of pastel colors.

It was pulled by what appeared to be a matched set of eight white horses whose tack gleamed in the sunlight with flashes of light that looked very much like rainbows. There were blue and pink and yellow and red flowers woven into the horses' combed manes. The carriage slowed to a stop right in front of me!"

"Who was in it?" Mickey demanded.

"I'm getting to that. Inside was a lady wearing a golden crown delicately inlaid with what looked like green jade. Her clothes were richly and colorfully embroidered. She wore a delicate necklace of the same jade as her crown and matching bracelets, which gave off the same rainbow light effects as I'd seen on her horses' decorations. A shawl, woven of the most beautiful purple and gold silk threads, held delicately to her shoulders and draped across each forearm.

"The inside of the carriage was also well upholstered in light purple velvet from the look of it. Connected to the window through which I saw the lady was a small delicate single-bud vase, and in it was a single yellow miniature rose. I was speechless in the presence of all this luxury."

Gina narrowed her eyes a bit as if wanting to see every aspect of her story clearly in her mind's eye. She continued, "The lady in the carriage looked at the rose, smiled, then looked at me, leaned a little out of the carriage window so I could hear her speak, and said, 'Tell me, dear, are you going to the party?'"

Gina said, "Of course, I was completely clueless. I mean, I had *no idea* what she was talking about. I gathered up my courage and said, after giving a small curtsey as it seemed the right thing to do, 'Ma'am, thank you for asking, but no. You see, I don't have an invitation.'

"The lady in the carriage smiled and gave a small, polite laugh and then said, 'What's your name, dear?'

"At this point, J.T. strode up beside me, gave the lady a magnificent bow, cleared his throat, and said, 'Beg pardon, My Queen. This is Princess Gina of Lemars. I apologize most sincerely for our delay. We are even now on our way to your palace to help celebrate your son's birthday!'

"The Queen nodded before saying to me, 'Please forgive me, Princess, but I'm not at all sure I've ever heard of Lemars.'"

Gina looked at her cousins and Gigi and said, "What else could I do? I was still totally clueless as to what in the world was going on here so I just played along and said, 'Your Majesty'—I wasn't quite sure if I should call her that but it didn't seem to bother her or J.T., so I went with it—'I just arrived this morning aboard my ship, the *Parasol*. Thank you so very much for the invitation to your son's birthday party.'

"The Queen said, 'No, no, Your Highness, I'd be most honored if you could attend the party. Please say you'll come?'"

Gina said, "The Queen looked at me and then at J.T. I saw him nod slightly out of the corner of my eye, so I took a deep breath to summon up all my courage and said, 'Yes, My Queen. I'd love to attend. Thank you very much!'

"Then the Queen offered me a ride in her carriage, so J.T. helped me get in and then stepped up onto the back of the carriage with the queen's footmen and rode along."

Gina paused. Gigi and Mickey were looking at her wide-eyed with interest in her unfolding story. Mandy was looking at Gina too, but inside she was kicking herself for having allowed Gina to grab the parasol from her in the attic. If it hadn't been for that, Mandy would have had this adventure, not Gina! But she kept quiet, waiting for Gina to continue.

Smiling, Gina spent the next twenty minutes describing how fabulous the birthday party was at the castle and how much she felt like a princess during the story. And all the while, Mandy thought crossly, *Parties, a queen, a castle—it should have been me in that story. Not fair!* To be honest, Mandy was only half-listening, hoping Gina would quit yakking, and maybe she'd get her turn to use the parasol too.

When Gina finally stopped talking, Mickey said, "Great story, Gina! Really cool about the castle and party and everything. But there's one thing you haven't explained yet... how did you get back here?"

"Well," said Gina, "as I said, the party went on all day. Then finally, the party wound down, and everyone was escorted out into the courtyard to be sent home.

"J.T. arrived to pick me up in the same splendid carriage in which I'd arrived with the Queen hours earlier. I noticed that there was another beautiful carriage beside ours. This one contained a pretty redheaded girl in a flowing yellow dress. She waved at me and said, 'Goodbye!' I told J.T. I'd just met her an hour or so ago and that she was fun to play with, but I never got her name. As J.T. covered me with a light purple velvet blanket, he told me she was Princess Helen of Remsen. I wanted to ask if he meant the same Remsen that Gigi lives in, but I was so tired I couldn't get the words out!

"Anyway," Gina said, "I closed my eyes during the carriage ride...and suddenly, I was back standing on the sidewalk as if nothing happened!"

Mandy said, "It's so weird. You were only in a trance for like ten minutes!"

"How can that be?" wondered Gina. "I was at the party for hours!"

"Maybe it's like *Back to the Future*," Mickey guessed. "Something to do with the space-time continuum."

Mandy sighed loudly. "Oh, Mickey, sometimes I think you are crazy."

"Me... crazy? Gina tells a story that some magic umbrella whisks her away to another time and place...and I explain time maybe moves faster in Storyworld than here—and *you* call *me* crazy? Geez!"

It got very quiet as the three kids looked at each other in amazement, and then at Gigi. She had a look of extreme satisfaction on her face. "I'm just so happy that it worked for you," Gigi said.

Mandy asked, "Gigi, I have to know! Did you ask a question when you used the parasol?"

"I did," Gigi said. "I was pretty scared the first time, so my question was pretty simple. My question was, how do I get back home?"

"What was the answer?" asked Gina.

Gigi smiled and said, "The story ends when you fall asleep."

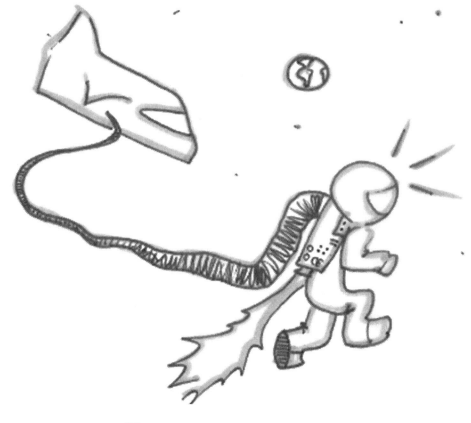

CHAPTER 3

THE NEXT QUESTION

G IGI STOOD UP AND clapped her hands. "Now, go back outside and play again before your grandma gets home."

The kids shuffled out with Gina still clutching the closed parasol. Once outside, they formed a small circle, and Mickey said, "So hey! It should be my turn! Let me try it! It is my birthday, you know!"

But Gina held the parasol away from him. "Mickey, your birthday was *last week*. I want to use it again; then, I'll let you try it."

"Wait! Who made you the boss of it?" Mickey said as he grabbed for the parasol.

Mandy watched, thinking, *This is how things always go. Gina tries to be bossy, and then Mickey tries to bully her into getting his way, and all the while, I'll probably end up giving in and letting them do what they want.* Mandy wanted this time to be different. She wanted to take a stand for what *she* wanted this time. Instead, she just watched the scene in front of her until she couldn't stand it anymore and shouted, "Stop it! You're going to break it!"

Mickey backed off, thrusting his hands into the front pockets of his blue jeans, turning his back on Gina, and hunching his shoulders. *That's how he always looks when he sulks,* Mandy thought.

Gina started strolling down the sidewalk, smiling triumphantly. She opened the parasol, put it on her shoulder, and spun it as she did before.

Nothing happened.

She looked up to make sure the sun was still shining and then tried walking faster. She tried twirling the parasol in either direction at different speeds. She worked the parasol on her other shoulder. She even tried walking backward, but *nothing happened.*

"Let me try," Mandy said. "Come on, please, Gina?"

Mickey shoved past her and said, "No, let me try now. It's my birthday, not Mandy's! Maybe you aren't doing it right." Gina closed the parasol and reluctantly gave it to Mickey, who broke into a huge grin. He began walking toward Gigi's backyard.

"Hey, Mickey!" Gina ordered. "Remember, you have to be walking in the sun to make it work!"

"Nope," he replied, "this thing is too girly for me to carry around town. I'm going to Gigi's backyard so no one else will see me. I'll use it there!"

"But you have to be walking and twirling the parasol like Gina did," protested Mandy, following him.

"J.T. didn't tell Gina that. He just said you need a sunny day," retorted Mickey.

And he kept walking.

Gigi's backyard was huge. It was surrounded by a hedge with dark green and yellow leaves. The hedge stood about five feet high, making the yard more-or-less private and out of sight from the average passerby.

In a far corner of the yard, the adults had created a fire pit and placed stumps as seats around it. During family get-togethers, the adults would gather around the fire pit, light a massive fire with fragrant oak logs, and as the flames danced and flowed, they'd tell stories, or talk amongst themselves, or sometimes even sing. Sometimes the kids got to roast large sweet-tasting marshmallows on long willow sticks—and even make s'mores!

Mickey sat on a stump with his back to the house. Gina approached him and said, "Mickey, wait just a minute, please? Let's first decide what question you should ask J.T., OK? Remember, you only get to ask one question, so this is important."

"Gina, I already know what I'm going to ask, OK? I got this!" he said defiantly. Gina sighed, shrugging her shoulders in acceptance of the situation. Mickey could be very stubborn when he wanted to be.

The girls sat on the other side of the fire pit, watching him. Mickey opened the parasol.

He sat there for a little while to see if anything would happen, but nothing did. Mickey started twirling the parasol on his shoulder. Then, in an instant, there was a flash of purple light, and *Mickey froze entirely still.*

On top of the parasol, the stone was gleaming bright purple.

Mandy, tearing her eyes from Mickey's frozen face, noticed the glowing of the stone and said to Gina, "Look! The stone! It's purple now. It was red when you were frozen."

The sound of a car coming up the gravel driveway caught Mandy's attention. She looked at the driveway, then at Mickey's frozen features, then at the glowing purple stone, and then at Gina and said softly, "Gina, look! Grandma's back. What are we going to do?"

Gina frowned for a moment. "Do nothing. Let's pretend we're sitting here talking. Mickey's back is toward her so she won't see that he's frozen, and she probably can't get a real good look at the glowing stone. Maybe... *maybe...* we'll be all right, and she won't notice anything."

Mandy nodded slowly in agreement.

Grandma stepped out of the car, her tiny feet making small crunching sounds as she walked. She moved around to the back of the car and unlocked the trunk. Then she stepped to the side of the car, waved at the kids, and called, "Girls, Mickey—come help me carry the groceries in!"

Mandy called back, "OK, Grandma. We'll be right there." Then she whispered to Gina, "I'll go, but you—take your time getting up. Stall a little."

Mandy headed toward Grandma at a slow walk. She glanced back to see Gina slowly rise and saunter after her.

"Mickey," Grandma called, "you come help, too! You can't make the girls do all of the work."

"We've got this, Grandma," Mandy said as she picked up a brown grocery bag and handed a gallon of milk to Gina.

But when Mickey didn't move, Grandma became instantly irritated. She walked toward Mickey and in a raised voice, said, "Mickey, I'm talking to you, and I expect you to pay attention when I speak to you. Do you hear me?"

Mandy, worried about what would happen next, held her breath as Grandma came within a little more than an arm's reach of Mickey. At that same moment, Mickey jumped off the stump, shouting, "That was so *cool*!"

Mickey turned and saw Grandma and then looked behind her at the girls. They were waving their hands, motioning to him to say nothing!

Mickey closed the parasol and then said, "Oh, sorry, Grandma! I was... I was... playing a game on my phone. I guess I didn't hear anything else. What did you want, Grandma?"

Grandma narrowed her ice blue eyes at him... but then relented from her impulse to snap at him for being woolly-headed and instead just said, "Mickey, please help the girls carry the groceries into the house so we can all enjoy our lunch."

"Sure thing, Grandma, happy to help," Mickey said as he trotted to the car. Gina whispered, "Good thinking, Mickey. That was close! Let's go eat lunch, and we can talk with Gigi later!" Mickey nodded in agreement.

As she carried her bags up the concrete stairs into the house, Mandy wondered if she would even get a chance to use the parasol now that Grandma was back.

During lunch, Grandma asked the kids what they were doing by the firepit. The kids looked at each other, not sure what to say, until Mickey, stuffing the last of his grilled cheese sandwich into his mouth, managed to say, "Oh, nothing much. We were taking turns playing this game I downloaded on my phone to see who would get the best score. It got hot out there, so I used the umbrella..."

"It's a parasol, Mickey," Gina corrected him as she licked Fig Newton from the fingers of her left hand.

"Whatever," Mickey continued. "So, I used the…" he glared at Gina, "*parasol* to give me some shade."

"Now kids," said Grandma, "be nice to each other. Finish your lunch. And, be sure to be very careful with that blamed parasol!"

After lunch, Grandma wanted to take a nap and then maybe watch Wheel of Fortune on TV. Gigi said she had napped while Grandma was getting groceries.

Gigi continued, "The kids and I will go outside on the porch so that we won't disturb your nap." She motioned the kids toward the front door.

Once they were all safely outside, Gigi sat on her favorite bentwood and cane rocking chair and said, "OK. Now, tell me what happened."

Mandy blurted out that Gina wouldn't share and tried to use the parasol again, but it wouldn't work. "Well… it sure worked for Mickey!" Gigi said. "Mickey, please tell us your story."

He began, "I was transported to outer space, which I thought was way better than going to some castle in the dark ages."

Gina hit him playfully on the shoulder.

Mickey continued, "Anyway, I was in a large space station that had huge windows all around. I could see Earth out one set of windows and the moon out another set. There were lots of people around me on the station, including this old guy who was standing at what looked like military attention right next to me."

"I'll just bet that was J.T.," Gina said.

Mickey said, "Yeah, it was J.T.! Now is it OK with you if I continue my story? Anyway, we were standing in some enormous docking bay, and there were smaller rocket ships, and escort crafts, and those kinds of things—and each ship was a different color. And—there was a purple ship named *Parasol*. Since J.T. and I had purple uniforms on, I figured that was my ship, and I began to walk slowly towards it.

"Just then, a girl with red hair and wearing a yellow uniform walked right by me and said, 'Hi!' For some reason, it kind of felt like I knew her…

"I was going to talk to her, but then some loud alarm went off, and a man's voice came over what must have been the public address system and announced, 'Captain Mickey, report to your ship immediately. Captain Mickey, please report to your ship. We have received a distress call from Mars, and we need you to investigate immediately!' Can you believe it? I was the captain of the ship!"

"So cool!" said Mandy, although inside she was still wondering when it would be her turn.

"Then what happened?" Gina asked.

"Then J.T. said, 'This way please, Captain,' and began to walk towards *Parasol*. While he walked, J.T. said, 'Captain, I'm your co-pilot. I'll review all the instruments and ensure the ship for takeoff.'

"Once our pre-flight was completed, J.T. said, 'Coupling tube engaged, Captain.' He then pushed a single gray button on *Parasol*'s dashboard, and this enormous transparent tube-like device rose up on all sides of the ship from the gleaming steel floor. The large tube rose up and over our ship and attached itself to what I thought was the ceiling of the space station.

"J.T. said, 'Atmosphere purging, Captain.' As soon as he said that, there was a terrific hissing sound, which I guessed was the air being vacuumed from the inside of the tube enclosing *Parasol*. 'Egress hatches opening, Captain,' J.T. said.

"Suddenly, what I thought was the ceiling began to retract, opening like a lens, and we were looking at the inky blackness of outer space with a million stars blazing in the darkness!

"J.T. said, 'Clear for takeoff, Captain.' He pushed a large green button on *Parasol*'s gleaming silver dashboard, and *Parasol* lifted off the deck and suddenly drove forward in a massive burst of speed—we were away and headed for Mars!"

"Just imagine—Mars!" Gigi exclaimed with a delighted smile.

"It was amazing," Mickey said. "The speed of *Parasol* was beyond belief! The Earth began shrinking, and the moon flashed by in the blink of an eye. Then I looked at the stars. They seemed to be getting stretched into long individual white lines. J.T. said, 'LightDrive engaged, Captain. We're now traveling at fifty percent of the speed of light. Mars arrival time is twenty-five minutes, Captain.'

"About twenty minutes later, J.T. approached my seat and said, 'Excuse me, Captain, but about that distress call? There are two scientists from NASA aboard an observation satellite studying Mars. We are now receiving reports that a small meteor has hit the satellite, and the scientists are running low on oxygen.'

"J.T. pushed a few more buttons on the control panel, sighed, and said, 'Sir, I did a sensor scan of the scientists' craft, and it appears the meteor has damaged the ship's docking mechanism, too. What that comes down to, Captain, is there is no way to rescue those two gentlemen and get them aboard our ship unless...'"

Mickey looked at Gigi and his cousins and said, "Suddenly, J.T. just stopped talking. I said, 'J.T., what is it? How can we save those scientists, it's our responsibility?'

"J.T. looked a little worried but finally said, 'Sir. The only way we can save those two scientists is if you... you...risk your life by executing a spacewalk from our ship to theirs. And—if the scientists have blacked out from low oxygen, you'll have to carry those gentlemen over.'

"I said, 'And if I don't try to save them?' And J.T. said, 'They'll have no chance, sir. No time for anyone else to get them at the rate their ship is losing oxygen.'

"'OK,' I told him. 'Let's do this!'"

"Oh, Mickey," said Gigi. "What a wonderful story you were in!"

"I know!" Mickey said. "Then J.T. handed me the parasol. And he told me to open it above my head. As soon as I did, it... well...*transformed* into a space helmet with a jet pack!

Then, J.T. pushed a bunch of buttons on the flat copper-colored control panel for the airlock door, and it started to glide open. I stepped into the airlock, and the door closed behind me. Quickly the atmosphere was bled from the airlock and the exterior door of *Parasol* slid open.

The only sound was the hissing of the oxygen in my now sealed helmet.

"I left the ship through the airlock and focused my eyes on the 'Visual Navigation Field'"—Mickey used air quotes here—"projected inside my helmet to steer me over to the Emergency Access Air Lock embedded in the side of the gleaming white NASA ship. The control panel next to the door was easy to figure out. It had only two buttons: Open and Close. I pressed the Open button, and the door opened. I entered the airlock, which sensed my presence and closed the door behind me. I watched the airlock atmosphere indicator change from red (no oxygen) to yellow (minimal oxygen present.)

"Another door now opened automatically. I could see inside the spaceship and I could see the scientists. Because the air inside the spaceship was so thin, the scientists were wearing their spacesuits. I approached them."

Mickey went on, "I read the names of the scientists from the labels on their spacesuits: Pete Graham and Sunil Rahuala. Over our suit communications link I said, 'Pete, I'm Mickey. I'm here to rescue you. Is there any other source of oxygen available on the ship?'

"Pete said, 'Yes, but the failing atmosphere has locked the door to the emergency supplies room. That's where our oxygen supply is. *And that's the room our laser weapons are in we'd use to cut the door to force it open!*'

"I said, 'Pete, take me to that room, now. I've got this!'

"The three of us moved swiftly down a series of narrow silver hallways before stopping in front of a red metal door that had the words 'Emergency Equipment' in large white block letters on it. I took my laser pistol—*Yes! I had a laser pistol!* —and used the power of its thin red shimmering beam to cut the door opening panel. As I'd planned, the heat from the laser defrosted the door-locking circuitry, and the door opened silently.

"We entered the room. The scientists led me across the gleaming silver metal floor to a large gray metal rack with a blue metal sign above it that read 'Emergency Atmospheric Equipment.' On shelves in the rack were green emergency oxygen cylinders.

"I spun each scientist around to access the fast emptying oxygen tanks on the backs of their spacesuits and activated the quick disconnect mechanism on top of each tank. Then I removed and swiftly replaced each tank."

Mickey said, "I told them, 'Those emergency tanks won't last long. We need to get you onto my ship, the *Parasol*, now!'"

"We ran back through the small maze of corridors, which were now noticeably colder and darker and made our way to the airlock. In just a couple of moments, we were safely back inside *Parasol*. Looking behind us at their abandoned craft, we noticed that the emergency lighting had now been used up and the scientists' ship was lifeless and dark."

Gina said, "Wow, that is just the most amazing rescue story!"

Mickey smiled, "You bet! After we were all safely inside *Parasol*, I walked to the captain's chair with its smooth brown leather and sat down. J.T. said, 'Orders, sir?'

"I said, 'Take us home, J.T. That's enough excitement for one day.'"

Gigi and the girls chuckled.

Mickey chuckled too and then added, "J.T. looked very happy and nodded. Then... then I must have dozed off on the way back and ended up here."

Mandy said, "Wow! How cool. That's a great story, Mickey!" Then she thought of something. "Wait...*wait... did you ask J.T. your parasol question?*"

"Yep," replied Mickey. "I asked why the magic didn't work for Gina when she tried it again. J.T. explained that the parasol might only be used once per day per person. That's a condition. The way J.T. explained it, the parasol is full of an *endless number of stories*. But those stories aren't just words on a page like most of the stories with which we're familiar. In this case, every one of these countless stories *is constantly changing, adapting, and, well, evolving!* They change *based on the person who experiences them.* That means *each story will be different each time it's experienced.* But you can get too much of a good thing, so the parasol only works once per day per user."

Yeah! Mandy thought. *I will get a turn after the others have had theirs. They can't hog it all the time.*

Gigi clapped in appreciation, and the girls joined in. "Oh, what a wonderful story, Mickey!" she said.

Suddenly, Grandma stuck her head out the front door and said, "What's with all of the applause?"

"Oh, nothing," said Gigi. "We need to talk. You kids play. I think it's Mandy's turn now."

CHAPTER 4

PHEF THE WIZARD

F *INALLY! MANDY THOUGHT AS* she clutched the parasol and raced off the white painted wooden porch. She hustled around the side of the house, cut a wide swath around Grandma's red and pink rose garden, and tore across the deep green backyard as fast as her black high-top Keds would carry her. Out of breath, she sat on one of the stumps and focused on catching her breath as Gina and Mickey approached.

Mickey sat beside Mandy, saying, "Boy, I wonder what your story will be! Bet it won't be as cool as going to outer space!"

Gina said, "Hey, Mandy, I've got a great idea for your J.T. parasol question."

Mandy ignored them both.

She opened the parasol and placed it on her shoulder. Just as she started twirling it, she heard the creak of the back door to the house open. Grandma rushed out, waving her arms and shouting, "Mandy, wait! Don't!"

Too late, it's my turn! Mandy thought.

A blue glow fell across her. Her vision blurred in the blue light. She felt like she was standing still… and spinning at the same time. Indistinct, blurred images appeared and disappeared in front of her, quickly fading away. She felt frustrated; she couldn't quite make out what the images were.

Finally, she found herself standing on a desolate hillside. Below spread an open vista of hundreds of acres of land covered in boulders. Across this landscape, large and small vents spewed steam, which condensed into shimmering silver, white, and blue water vapor rising into the stark blue sky.

Turning to her right, Mandy saw a large unevenly formed mountain some distance away. On top of the mountain sat what appeared to be an old stone castle with massive parapets and what Mandy thought was… a drawbridge.

There were some… creatures flying around the castle and in between the fortifications and towers.

"I wonder what those are," Mandy said aloud, squinting her dark hazel eyes to try and make out their shapes.

Behind Mandy, a deep bass voice loudly said, "Oh… no! How did we get to Talon?"

Mandy turned and saw a large man dressed in a vibrant blue robe. The robe had streaks of reds and purples in it that almost appeared electric in the bright sun. Looking down at her clothing, Mandy noticed she too was wearing a blue robe like this person.

Mandy said, "You must be J.T., as in Just The Valet. Right?"

J.T. bowed slightly and said, "At your service, Miss Mandy." Suddenly J.T.'s expression changed to one of shock. Looking past and behind Mandy, he bowed again, this time very profoundly, and said, "Greetings, Master!"

Mandy turned. Standing about a dozen paces behind her was a tall, ancient man. His long beard was as white and neatly combed as his snow-white waist-length hair. He wore a strikingly bright white robe and highly polished red shoes. He held a long, thick staff with a large stone on top. The stone glowed. It looked mostly blue. But as Mandy looked on, it showed so many colors in any one second that it was genuinely impossible to tell just exactly what color the stone was.

"Mandy, my dear," the man said softly but with great emotion, "how on Earth did you enter Talon?"

Mandy shot a glance at the parasol in her hand, considering for a moment before replying, "Uh, I don't know. To be honest, I don't even know what... or where... Talon is!"

The man frowned and looked down toward his feet as if he were considering the myriad of small rocks strewn on the deep brown soil. With a massive intake of breath, he straightened, glanced at J.T., looked at Mandy, and said, "Follow me."

He began to walk in the direction of the castle.

Over his right shoulder, he said, "Talon is the center and the core of Storyworld. It is here that my magic endures to power the parasol and its countless stories for children."

He stopped and turned to look intently at Mandy. "This is most...troubling. You see, no one was to enter this realm. I placed defenses in my spell to prevent anyone besides myself and J.T. from coming here. I hate to bear bad tidings, but we must investigate this at once—if you are ever to return home."

Mandy felt a chill of fear.

Stay here, stuck, forever? she thought. *Never see Gigi's smiling face again... or my parents... or my cousins?* Questions raced through her mind. In a split second, before she was about to speak up and ask one of the questions, she realized who the older man was.

Mandy said softly but with wonder, "You're... Phef, the wizard, aren't you?"

"Indeed, I am," he replied. "Before my body died, I transported my essence into this world and beyond, and using the ancient spells, I was able to reconstitute myself here as you see me now."

As Mandy listened, she watched as the old man, who seemed quite real and substantial one second, momentarily turned transparent, and she could see right through him. Then, a fraction of a second later, he'd appear solid again.

The wizard continued, "I exist now on several planes of dimensional existence, this being just one of them. But in this way, my thinking was that my dear Blanchetta would be able to continue to enjoy my stories.

"Alas, I was hasty and didn't foresee that the spells would only work at her current age ... ten. The very second she turned eleven," and here he shook his great head and cast a heavy sigh, "the enchantment for the parasol no longer worked for her."

Phef looked at J.T. Both nodded as the wizard said, "Only a ten-year-old child can use the parasol to enter Storyworld."

He smiled and looked around him with a sweeping arm gesture that seemed to take in that spot and the whole realm around them. "And so it was that I was able to enchant this realm to keep this dimension of existence of me—and my magic—alive, forever."

Mandy nodded, still unsure of the tale being told by the wizard who kept sliding in and out of focus in front of her.

Phef said, "And that is why the parasol still works for you, Mandy, hundreds of years after I left your world." He dropped his voice to a somber note and continued, "But that is also... why I am most worried about your return."

"What do you mean?" Mandy said. Her voice wavered. Fear filled the corners of her eyes. "I can get back home, right?"

J.T. moved silently next to her. He patted her head and said softly, "Together, we will figure something out. You see, part of the enchantment of Talon is that one can never tire and fall asleep here. This ensures that my Master Phef's magic will always be available to power Storyworld."

Mandy brightened a bit but then thought of something. She said to J.T., "So...but, umm...if I can't fall asleep, I can't... return home. Right?"

Phef smiled at Mandy and spoke, "You are a clever little witch, aren't you? I need to study this problem. Now, we must get to my castle immediately."

Mandy heard J.T. snap the thick heels of his shiny black knee-high boots together and say, "Yes, My Master."

She looked toward the castle. To get there meant navigating a very steep hillside with hundreds of jagged rocks and boulders, not to mention the white-hot steam vents. She wondered aloud, "How are we going to get up there?"

Phef gave a small deep chuckle and said, "We will fly, of course." He raised his arms, the arms of his pure white robe sliding back across the pale skin of his forearms. Holding his staff high, Phef pointed it, closed his eyes, and began speaking very softly in a language Mandy couldn't understand.

She looked to see where the wizard's staff was pointing and saw two of the flying creatures up by the castle turn... and begin to fly down toward them.

They moved with astonishing speed. It seemed like mere seconds before the rhythmic movement of their gigantic wings stirred the air by Mandy. As they got close, Mandy jumped to stand closer to J.T. for safety. He chuckled, but his muscular arms moved with surprising delicacy to protect her. She closed her eyes as the gigantic flying creatures grew ever closer.

But then her curiosity took over. She peeked through almost closed eyelids and watched as two...yes! They had to be! DRAGONS! ... landed on the ground...*in front of Phef!*

Phef walked to the most massive dragon. Its bulk was so vast it blotted out the sun in front of Mandy. The dragon lowered its enormous head toward Phef, sending out hot breath from its large twin nostrils. The nails of the dragon's feet were sunk nearly two feet into the dark soil. The lids of the great beast's eyes were narrow slits, the eyes themselves a bright piercing green. The dragon's scales were a beautiful deep golden color.

Mandy thought, *From end-to-end, this beast is bigger than my school bus! Yet it clearly is under the absolute control of Phef!*

Phef gently stroked the dragon's forehead. "This is Paction. She is the queen of the dragon herd in Talon." He winked at J.T. and went on, "Oh... and the little blue one over there is her son, Vito."

Vito snorted at this pronouncement and little balls of flame the size of tennis balls flew from his twin nostrils.

"Steady, Vito," J.T. said. The little dragon looked embarrassed.

Phef climbed aboard Paction by using the dragon's huge front leg as a step. He reached for Mandy. "You'll ride with me. J.T., you go with Vito."

Phef took Mandy's hand, guiding her up onto the dragon. As he did so, he motioned to Mandy to hand him the parasol. Pausing just briefly, she did. As soon as Phef's hand closed around the handle of the parasol, it transformed into a small, eighteen-inch-long version of Phef's staff. The stone at the end of the staff remained a bright blue.

"J.T., keep this safe for now," he ordered, and the small staff floated from his hand into the palm of J.T.'s black-gloved hand.

All Mandy could manage to say was, "Wow." She sat directly behind the wizard. This was odd as one minute she saw him, right there in front of her, and the next minute it seemed as if he were gone. Very bizarre.

The feeling of the giant golden-hued dragon breathing beneath her was mesmerizing.

With a gentle nudge from Phef, Paction slowly stood up. Mandy had a distinct impression of almost limitless strength as the massive beast flexed herself. Its enormous wings unfolded and stretched, shining in the sun. They radiated a rainbow of colors: gold, blue, red, orange, and even a pale green as the great beast flapped her wings and lifted effortlessly into the air.

"The castle, Paction," said Phef. Mandy could swear she caught a nod from the dragon's head.

As the dragon flew higher, Mandy could see across the whole domain: volcanoes, rivers, and mountains dotted the landscape for what must have been hundreds of miles—almost as far as the eye could see. As they moved in the general area of the castle, she saw that it wasn't surrounded just by rocks and crags. Instead, it was in the center of a village with people and animals scurrying around.

"How did all those people get here?" Mandy asked.

"They are simply part of the realm," Phef explained. "Living completely alone for eons would drive any person crazy. These folks are here to make my endless life more normal."

Mandy nodded. Then she gathered her courage to ask a question she wasn't *quite* sure she wanted to be answered. "Phef... umm... why did you call me a witch?"

The wizard laughed out loud. "Ho! It's no great mystery, girl. People of magic are called wizards if they are a boy, or witches if they are a girl. That should come as no surprise to you."

Mandy shrugged her shoulders in agreement.

"The part you may find intriguing, though, Mandy, is this," Phef said. "You, my dear, are a part of my bloodline—you are my direct descendant. Therefore, you are *of magic*—and thus a witch. You see, Mandy, the parasol won't work for just anyone. The user of the parasol must be from *my magical bloodline*, just like Blanchetta. And just like you."

Mandy was stunned into silence at the old wizard's words. She felt numb, and there was a faint ringing sound in her ears. She thought, *Magical? Descendant? Bloodline? Me? Cool! And... and... awesome! Wait until I get to tell my story to the others! That is if I can get home again!*

This last thought was too awful to dwell on, so Mandy tightened her grip around Phef's there-then-gone-then-there-again waist and kept thinking, *I am a witch!*

The old man interrupted her thoughts. "Now, hold on tight, Mandy! Landings can be a bit... fun!"

Mandy wasn't quite sure what to think of that until she felt the dragon, with no discernable effort, come to a dead stop—*in midair*. The massive beast then let loose with an enormous roar. Small red, white, and orange balls of fire flew from its nose.

Mandy felt a great shudder of tremendous muscular strength pass through the body of the dragon. Then, in what Mandy was sure was just *two* flaps of its golden curtain-like wings, the dragon was sitting on the ground. It had landed in an open courtyard at the top level of the castle.

"That was *awesome!*" Mandy blurted. Phef nodded his head.

The dragon yawned and extended its right front leg so its passengers could descend to the ground.

Once they were down, Phef absently patted the dragon on the nose and then walked quickly across the fertile brown soil of the courtyard toward the gray and dark stone monolith that was his castle, just thirty or so yards away.

Mandy had almost to run to keep up with the older man. She heard the steady footfalls of J.T. close behind her.

Passing through a sizeable rounded entryway in one wall of the castle, the wizard hurried to a massive sand-colored stone staircase, his red shoes making soft scuffling sounds as he descended step after step and staircase after staircase. The stone walls and ceilings glowed yellow and gold from the fiery radiance of large wooden torches set into stone holders along the stairways.

Mandy had no idea how far they had descended. A hundred feet? Five hundred?

Finally, after many more minutes, they reached the bottom of the last staircase. Mandy was breathless. J.T. quietly stepped next to her. They both walked the remaining ten to twelve feet to join Phef at the center of the large, round room. Mandy looked around at the shimmering white walls.

Phef thrust his staff toward a neat hole in the rock floor of the room. With a small bright blue flash, the staff froze about two inches above the hole. He let go of the staff—and it stood stock-still, hanging there in midair.

Phef then closed his eyes, raised his arms, and began to chant. Mandy recognized it as the same language he used earlier.

Mandy froze, eyes wide open as the floor began to rotate. Her eyes grew even wider as the floor began to descend, like an elevator. The torches in their wall holders grew dimmer and smaller, and it became very dark in the room. The one bright spot was from the glow of the stone at the top of Phef's staff.

With a jolt, they and the room came to a stop. At the same instant, the wall directly in their front moved to the left, with a soft rumbling sound until a doorway was formed, which led into a room.

"Welcome to my sanctum," Phef said, and with one great sweeping motion, he waved them toward the doorway. Mandy slipped her small hand into J.T.'s gloved hand as she moved toward the room.

Inside, large copper-colored vats with steam and bubbles rising from them stood sentry around the perimeter of the room. The fire didn't so much burn as glow beneath the vats. Opposite sat a long wooden table made of dark wood. On it was an assortment of vials in different colors, candles tall and short, and various types of small green plants.

In the middle of the sanctum, a shower of golden droplets fell from a dimly lit round opening in the ceiling. Mandy noticed that the golden droplets ranged in size from almost invisible to as large as a grape. She also saw, and this amazed her, that the golden droplets fell at different speeds, and some even seemed to slow—even stop—on their voyage down to a large copper basin on the floor. The droplets made a soft *pat-pat* sound as they hit the surface film inside the basin.

Breaking the silence, Phef said, "I need you to get into the Shower of Illumination." When he saw Mandy's look of concern, he added, "Fear not, it will not hurt you, nor even get you wet." She looked at J.T., who nodded reassuringly.

Phef led Mandy to the edge of the shower of golden droplets. He held his hand in the shower for a few seconds. "See, nothing to fear," he said.

Mandy took a long deep breath, looked Phef straight in the eye, and, without moving her gaze, extended her arm slowly into the shower.

She froze in place, only moving her eyes to observe her arm.

The droplets went *around* her arm—without touching her skin! And they turned *blue* as they passed her arm. She felt drawn to the droplets and slowly moved all of herself into their stream.

As she watched, the entire shower began to change its glow from gold to blue.

Phef paced around the shower, looking into it and studying Mandy from all angles. Finally, he motioned for her to come out. Mandy noticed the wizard had been right, she was as dry as a bone!

Solemnly, Phef said, "For those of us that are of magic, our capabilities in magic strengthens as we grow from baby to adult, reaching its peak in adulthood. For most of us, Mandy, that evolution takes a long time."

The old wizard smiled. "But with you, my dear little witch—your inner magic is already powerful."

"It is?" Mandy whispered in awe.

The old man lifted his staff and held it at arm's length, the whiteness of his sleeves reflecting the glow from the droplets. "See this, at the top of my staff?"

Mandy looked at the stone, which still seemed mostly blue but whose color changed, almost appearing to vibrate with colors.

Phef said, "This is my dragonstone. It has a sister stone which is located at the top of the parasol. Both dragonstones were forged from the flames of Paction's dragon breath. When our inner magic is channeled through a dragonstone, we can create spells and enchantments and use our magic out in the world."

"I think I understand," Mandy said, trying to sound more confident than she felt. "But what does that have to do with me coming here? And, how will I get home?"

"Ah, two outstanding questions," Phef answered. "The parasol and the dragonstone work together to *sense* the presence, or lack of presence, of the inner magic of the person holding the parasol. The dragonstone uses the infinite power of the sun to tap or channel or access that magic. And one way it does that is to transport an individual to Storyworld."

Mandy nodded as the old man went on. "Now, since your magic, Mandy, is so strong, I believe the dragonstone thought you were me and mistakenly brought you to Talon."

Mandy smiled. "I see. And home...?"

The old man lowered his voice to a softer pitch. "Yes. As to your second question, well... ahem. I'm afraid that you won't be able to leave."

Mandy felt panic grip her stomach.

Phef said, "As a safeguard in keeping my magic controlled and functioning in Talon, I'm afraid there is no spell, no incantation, no potion which I can use to put you to sleep."

Mandy wanted to say something, anything, but she was quite simply gripped by fear.

The wizard reached over to pat Mandy's chestnut brown hair and said, "There's more, I'm afraid. Alas, my darling, as you stay here, you will remain frozen in time back in your world."

Mandy stared at Phef for a long moment. Then she sat down on a stool and began to cry.

J.T. crouched next to her. She threw her arms around his neck and sobbed, "I don't want to stay here forever. I want to go home!"

Phef moved closer and stoked Mandy's hair. "My darling ... you are welcome to stay here with me. There are children in the village! You can play with them all you like. There's even a school for you. You could read and study and do all the things a girl like you would do."

"A…a school?" Mandy said as she wiped tears from her face.

With a puzzled look, Phef responded hopefully, "Yes, there is a school. Does that please you?"

"Maybe," said Mandy. "J.T., can you take me there?"

"Of course, Miss Mandy," said J.T. as he stood to attention. "Anything you like."

Mandy sighed. *What I'd like,* she thought, *is to be back in Gigi's kitchen, eating fresh oatmeal and raisin cookies and drinking a nice glass of milk before Mom gets back from shopping. I want to be back in my world. This is all so confusing!*

A fresh wave of tears spilled down her cheeks.

"Now there, Miss Mandy," said J.T., "I think I have just the cure for those tears! Let's go make some new friends for you!" He smiled a dazzlingly white smile at Mandy, who nodded.

Wiping her eyes on her sleeve, Mandy stood up, took a deep breath, and followed J.T. toward the village. She could hear the school's bell ring and saw it swinging in the distance in what must have been the school's bell tower.

It took about ten minutes to reach the school. As Mandy and J.T. walked, people they passed in the village all seemed to know J.T. well and voiced greetings.

And there it was, the schoolhouse. Just as Phef had said, it *was* a real school—right down to the bell tower with sunlight glinting off the silver bell. Children of all ages ran here and there.

Entering the schoolhouse through the red double doors in front, Mandy walked down the brown oak floors of the main hall. She stood on tiptoes to peek into the rectangular windows set into each of the brightly colored classroom doors. Next to each door sat a bookcase stuffed with books. The smell of books, paper, pencil shavings, watercolor paint, floor wax, and even milk flooded over her, as she explored the school.

Mandy walked to the open door of a classroom. Several students were seated at rows of desks. The teacher, a pleasant-looking man, walked up to Mandy and said, "You must be J.T.'s friend. Why don't you join us? We're going to be learning some fun math today."

Mandy turned and looked at J.T., who nodded and said, "This is Mr. Cooper, he'll take good care of you. I'll wait out here, Miss Mandy." He eased his bulk into a small blond-colored wooden chair next to the doorway. Mandy was sure that if it could, that chair would have groaned under his weight.

She smiled at the teacher and said, "I'll be right back." She walked to J.T. and leaned very close to his ear. She whispered. J.T. nodded. He glanced over his shoulder at Mr. Cooper and then turned his massive head to whisper into Mandy's ear. After a long moment, she nodded. J.T. looked her in the face and smiled.

Then the teacher led Mandy to a walnut-colored desk and chair. A rectangular green book with *"Love Your Math!"* by Felix Cooper splashed across the front sat squarely on a small stack of scratch paper. Two yellow pencils with green erasers nestled next to the book.

Mr. Cooper said, "Class, this is Mandy. Please make her feel at home. OK, let's get into today's lesson, formula word problems!"

Mandy thought Mr. Cooper made word problems about as fun and exciting as they could ever be, but eventually, just like at home, after a while... Mandy... got... so... bored... she... fell asleep.

When Mandy opened her eyes next, she was sitting on a stump, and Gigi, Grandma, Gina, and Mickey were all staring at her anxiously.

"Oh, thank goodness!" said Grandma, leaping to her feet as fast as her aged legs would allow. She hugged Mandy close, stroking her hair. "I tried to stop you, but you didn't hear me. I got so scared when you were frozen solid. None of us, not even all of us, could move you! But now you're back! And, you're OK, right?"

I'm safely home, after all, Mandy thought. *And... I'm a witch!* A grin of relief and excitement tugged at her lips.

"She's fine, Grandma," Mickey said. "But danged if you weren't gone for almost two hours!"

"Oh, Mickey, you always exaggerate!" laughed Gina. "It was longer, but still, only about a half-hour. We were worried, but all's well that ends well."

"So," said Gigi. "Tell us what happened."

Mandy stole a furtive look at Grandma, who nodded and said, "It's all right, child. I know, I know."

Mandy took in a deep breath, settled herself on the stump, and retold her story right down to the moment when she fell asleep in Mr. Cooper's math class. She laughed and said, "Phef, the wizard, thought of pretty much everything he could think of so no one would get tired in Talon... but he didn't plan on boredom, I guess."

Everyone laughed, even Grandma. Gigi laughed so hard her shoulders moved up and down like an old water pump, which made everyone laugh even harder.

Finally, Mickey quit laughing enough to ask, "Did you remember to ask J.T. your parasol question?"

As Mandy got control of her laughter, she said, "I did. I asked him why the parasol never worked for Grandma. He said it *only* works if there are four family generations alive at the same time. When Phef created the parasol—just for his magic bloodline—he was Blanchetta's great-grandfather. His son, Blanchetta's grandfather, and his granddaughter, Blanchetta's mother, were also alive. So right now, we three cousins have Gigi, Grandma, and our parents—*four generations of magic!*"

"So, that's why it never worked for me!" Grandma stated. "My grandparents had passed on before I was even born." She looked up at the deep blue sky. "Oh, Mom, I'm sorry I never believed your stories about the parasol. But I sure do now!"

Mandy turned to her grandmother, whose ice blue eyes twinkled. "I'm sorry, Grandma. I wish you could have experienced this too."

Grandma gave Mandy a big hug and said, "That's all right, my dear. I'm so happy it works for you three. And that it will work for all your brothers and sisters when they turn ten, too. This is so amazing I can't believe it's real."

CHAPTER 5

THANKSGIVING

GIGI, GRANDMA, AND THE cousins sat around the fire pit for hours. They talked about the parasol, and the magic rules, and retold their stories for each other's enjoyment.

As the day wound down, each of the kids wanted to take the parasol home, and they argued as to who should get it. Finally, Gigi decided the parasol should stay at her house, but that the children could come over and use it as often as they wanted. She suggested naming the fire pit the "Circle of the Parasol" and said, "This is the perfect place to use the parasol and retell your stories to the rest of us."

Everyone, even Grandma, nodded their agreement.

Finally, the kids and Grandma said goodbye to Gigi and piled into Grandma's car. When they arrived at Grandma's house, the cousins' moms were already there waiting for them.

When they walked into the brightly lit kitchen, Mandy's mom said, "Where have you been? We've been here for an hour! I called your cell, Mom, but you never answered!"

At first, everyone just looked at each other. Then, all at once, the kids started talking. It grew so loud no one could make any sense of what anyone else was saying. Finally, Grandma shushed the whole group and told her daughters to sit down because there was something vital for them to hear.

Once everyone settled down, Grandma looked from one adult to another, gazing at them squarely in the eyes and saying nothing.

Grandma began to speak. Very softly yet clearly, she told them about the parasol. Then she told them about each kid's adventure in Storyworld. No one else spoke a word until she was done. And when she finished, the only sound in the room was the soft hum of the air conditioner.

Finally, Gina's mom said, her voice starting low and building to a crescendo, "What is going on, Mom? You're talking like this all happened!"

Gina was on her feet in a heartbeat, "It's true, Mom! I really went to Storyworld. And I really spent a day at a birthday party in a castle."

"And I went to outer space," insisted Mickey.

Mandy's mom stood up and walked to the doorway, her outline framed by the soft glow of the setting sun showing in the doorway. "No. No! This can't be true! Come on, Mandy! We are going home."

"Joy, sit back down!" Grandma snapped in a tone that brooked no nonsense and caused her daughter to swallow hard ... and do as she was told.

Again, Grandma looked at each adult in the eyes before speaking. She pointed at each with the index finger of her right hand. "Tomorrow is Sunday. You will all bring your entire families to Gigi's house for lunch. After that, the kids will demonstrate how the parasol works. I will call your brother and have him come, too. That way, the whole family will all be in the know about the parasol. And that's the way ... *it ... will ... be!*"

Then, with a curt nod of her head, Grandma turned to the children. She threw open her arms, "Come. Come here and give me a big hug goodbye, my dears. Today was so special, and I'm so happy for you."

One by one, the kids did as she asked. Then the families each clustered together and walked out of the room, across the parlor, and out of the house into a crisp evening.

Once in the car, Mandy tried to talk to her mom about the parasol, but her mother kept an iron grip on the big steering wheel, stared straight ahead into the lonely road in front of her—and shook her head no.

Finally, she erupted, "This whole story of a magical umbrella is so far-fetched. So fantastic. Such *nonsense!* I can't believe that Grandma went along with you to make all this up and is still acting like it's true! How could she? How COULD she?"

"But it *is* true!" Mandy insisted sulkily. "What have I ever done to make you think I would invent such a story? Invent such a lie? What? And *how* could I convince everyone else—and Grandma, too—to go along? How COULD I?"

There was silence in the car broken only by the purr of the car engine and the sound of the tires on the pavement.

Mandy folded her arms over her chest and chewed on her lip. *Fine!* she thought. *Fine! If Mom doesn't believe me, I won't talk to her.* She didn't say another word for the rest of the ride home. She didn't even reply when Mom asked what she'd like for dinner, or if she wanted to watch a movie with her later.

After her mom had parked the car in the large cluttered garage, pushed on the squeaky parking brake, and turned off the engine, Mandy bolted from the car and into the house, slamming the garage door behind her. She ran down the carpeted hallway, up the carpeted stairs to the second floor, and down another carpeted hallway to her room. She slammed that door, too.

For her part, her mother knew when to leave well enough—such as it was—alone.

Mandy changed out of her play clothes and into a pink and white nightshirt, jumped into her cozy bed, pulled the blue bedspread up under her chin, and cried herself to sleep, all the while thinking that she didn't understand why her mom wouldn't believe her. Or trust in her.

The next day, Mandy was startled awake by a shake of her shoulder. It was her dad. He said, "Wake up, Bebita. We're going to go to church. And then we're going to drive to Gigi's to get this whole parasol thing sorted out."

"You believe me, don't you, Papi?" pleaded Mandy as she rubbed her eyes.

Mandy's father sighed. "I'm not sure what to believe. If I told you such a story, would you believe me?"

"I'd believe anything you said if you swore it was true!" said Mandy, and she jumped out of bed and ran across the room to the bathroom. Predictably, she slammed the door.

Mandy was silent for the rest of the morning. She perked up once they got into the car after church. Mandy's sister, Evie, leaned over and whispered, "I believe you, Mandy. I can't wait to hear about the next place you visit in Storyworld."

Mandy gave her a big smile and then started thinking about being a witch. *If I'm a witch, then no one can boss me around. I'd be able to do spells and stuff. Then maybe Mom will treat me like I'm all grown up instead of like a little kid! Next time I go to Storyworld, I'll get my own dragonstone so I can use magic whenever I want to.*

Mandy's family was the last to arrive at Gigi's. When Mandy got out of the car, she noticed dark gray and black storm clouds approaching from the west. She hoped they'd all get to use the parasol before it started raining. Walking across the expansive green yard, she saw her aunts, uncles, and cousins were already sitting around the fire pit. Most were on stumps, but some of the adults sat in fold-up camping chairs.

Mandy saw Gina, also seated on a stump, holding the parasol. *Figures,* she thought. *Gina always gets to go first!*

"Hurry up, Mandy!" Gina called. "We want to go before the storm gets here!"

Mandy's dad set up two brown canvas camping chairs for him and her mom to sit on. Her mom said, "OK. We're here. Let's get this farce going so we can settle this once and for all and get back home!"

Gina opened the parasol, placed it over her right shoulder, and twirled it as a yellow shaft of sunshine lit the dragonstone. Smiling, she stuck one leg into the air, and with a flash of red light, she froze solid. *Show off!* Mandy thought.

Gina's mom bolted out of her chair, screaming, *"Oh my God!"* The other parents hurried to Gina's side and tried to move her or pick her up, but she wouldn't budge.

Mandy thought it was rather comical, watching them as they tried to (a) deal with a "frozen" Gina, and (b) believe what was happening right in front of their eyes.

After ten minutes of pandemonium, (including one uncle suggesting he get his bulldozer to take Gina to the nearest hospital), there was a flash of red light from the dragonstone, and Gina's leg moved back to a normal sitting position.

Gina looked at the adults, all frozen in place now themselves at the sight of Gina moving, and said, "See—we told you the parasol was magical."

All the adults dissolved into a cacophony of talking, questioning, and demanding.

Gina closed the parasol and climbed up onto her stump. She put her hands on her hips and said, "Everybody be quiet! I'm going to tell you about my new story now. Are you going to listen or keep babbling?" She eyed the looming rain clouds.

It took the adults a couple of minutes to settle down, but curiosity, as they say, killed the cat, and it surely killed their desire to whine.

Mandy, on the other hand, only half-listened as Gina described soaring over Paris, France, in a hot air balloon. Mandy was focused on thinking about how to talk to J.T. about getting a dragonstone. She didn't think he would approve, so she thought the smart path might be to be patient, casually ask questions here and there, and not raise suspicions. She nodded to herself, that would be her plan during *her* next visits to Storyworld.

Gina had barely wrapped her story up when Mandy stood up and put her hand out, "My turn. May I please have the parasol, Gina?"

But before Gina even held it out to give to Mandy, those ominous clouds Mandy had seen let loose, and a thunderstorm rolled in and rain pelted down. Amid the smell of damp earth and rainwater, everyone scrambled toward the house, trying to avoid fast-filling puddles turned brown by the fertile ground below.

Once inside, Gina handed the parasol to Gigi and said, "Guess there won't be any more Storyworld trips today, huh?"

Gigi nodded. Mandy fumed.

Over the next couple of hours, the parents, wanting to know every detail, peppered the kids with question after question: How could this be possible? Who helped you? Do you feel OK, no, aftereffects? Are you sure it's not radioactive? Maybe it causes cancer. Is this hypnosis? Drugs?

Over time, the kids grew bored with answering one variation or another of the same questions over-and-over-and-over.

Finally, the parents accepted that the kids were safe and that they looked fine. But they decided they would make *darn sure* they knew in advance before anyone went on another of these "adventures!" After a long while, the family turned to a discussion of how often they would come to Gigi's house.

As it turned out, both Mickey and Gina had summer sports teams that would keep them busy for the balance of July. Mandy's younger sister played soccer three nights a week, as well. Mandy wasn't into sports, and her plan—up to this point—had been to pretty much just stay at home and watch TV. But now she begged her parents to let her stay at Gigi's house for the rest of the summer.

"Oh no, Mandy," said her mom, "that would be too much for Gigi."

Then Grandma interceded. "Joy, I think this would be wonderful for Mandy. I'll come and stay here with Gigi too—and help watch over Mandy. That way, I can supervise her use of the parasol until school starts. You can come to visit on the weekends."

Grandma turned to the rest of the parents. "Laina, you can bring Mickey any day or weekend that it works for you. And Lilah, since you have the summer off from your teaching, you can bring Gina any day that she doesn't have a game."

The kids all looked at each other out of the corners of their eyes, and subtly nodded agreement. Mandy then looked at her mother with pleading eyes.

"Fine," Mandy's mom reluctantly said. But she insisted that they go home first, and she would bring Mandy back later in the week. The other parents agreed to a test weekend. "And then we'll see," they seemed to say in unison.

This led to a group discussion (some might say argument) about making plans for bringing food and drinks and turning each weekend into a big family get-together. Mandy's uncle Tyler started calling the three cousins 'The Magic Tweens' and said each weekend would be "The Magic Tween Show." Mandy and her cousins got a big kick out of this.

Mickey said, "Grandma, you should record our stories on your phone and save them and then send everyone a link to the file, that would be cool. That way, we'll know what's going on even if we aren't at Gigi's house when it happens."

"Umm, yeah. Sure. Good idea, Mickey," said Grandma, slowly and none too confidently. "But... you better show me how to do that before you leave!"

And so, it went.

Mandy spent the rest of the summer at Gigi's, taking advantage of every possible sunny day. Weekends at Gigi's became a whirlwind of family gatherings, with the Magic Tween Show taking center stage, followed by bonfires and cookouts around the newly christened "Circle of the Parasol."

The younger cousins were excited every time the parasol was used. They couldn't wait until they were ten years old and could use it themselves.

As for Mandy, throughout her visits to Storyworld, she worked on her plan. Here and there, she asked J.T. questions about the nature of dragonstones, explaining, "I want to understand more about the history of Phef's magic."

Gradually, Mandy learned. She knew from her previous conversation with Phef that dragonstones are forged by a dragon's fiery breath. From J.T., she discovered that the dragonstones' main ingredient consisted of one or more items from a carefully gathered list of precious metals. He also taught her that for a dragonstone to work for a certain witch or wizard, it had to also contain something special, something of great personal, or intrinsic, or emotional value to that person.

At first, this puzzled Mandy. She didn't think she owned anything "valuable" or "special." She thought about the contents of her ballerina jewelry box. She had friendship bracelets that were *pretty* special to her—but they were made of beads and thread, not metal. She did own a broken chain of real gold, so that was valuable. But she'd found it in the grass of the baseball diamond, and it just wasn't *that* special to her.

For days Mandy was puzzled: how could she get her dragonstone?

Then, two weeks before school started, Mandy returned to her parents' house to prepare for her family's vacation trip to the Black Hills of South Dakota. As she was packing, something hanging from the dresser mirror in her bedroom caught her eye: it was a solid silver cross on a braided silver chain. *My baptism gift from Gigi! Silver is a precious metal! And... I loved that Gigi gave it to me for such an important and special occasion,* she thought. *I'll start wearing this always from now on. Then all I need to do is find a dragon in Storyworld—and I'll ask him to make me a dragonstone!*

Mandy's new plan was set.

Once school started, the families met at Gigi's house on Sundays after church. After a break for lunch, the parents would supervise while one or another of the Magic Tweens used the parasol.

Mandy was excited each time it was her turn to use the magic—but each time, she was disappointed because none of the stories she experienced included dragons. She began to wonder if only the Talon realm had dragons. Since Phef had changed his safeguards to prevent her from reentering Talon, it might be possible *she'd never even see a dragon again!* The thought terrified her.

As the year headed toward its end, Mandy noticed that Gina was quieter than usual. "What's up?" Mandy asked one afternoon as they cleaned the fire pit.

"I'm turning eleven soon," Gina said quietly. "My birthday is on the Sunday after Thanksgiving. Then... then... the parasol... won't work for me anymore."

Mandy was sympathetic to Gina's situation. It would be hard to give up the parasol—*just because of a stupid birthday!*

She said, "I understand, Gina."

Thinking about birthdays made her think about her cousin Danny, Uncle Tyler's son. He would turn ten in November.

Danny was so excited about the idea of using the parasol that he couldn't seem to stop talking about getting his turn to use it. His parents had even planned a big birthday party at Gigi's house to celebrate his first visit to Storyworld.

But, the Thursday before the party, Danny went to the hospital and had to have his appendix removed in an emergency operation that was just in the nick of time to save his life! So, Danny stayed in the hospital for a few days and, naturally, none of the families went to Gigi's house—they choose to visit Danny.

The adults decided that they would reschedule Danny's birthday party for the day after Thanksgiving. Everyone would stay at Gigi's house for the entire holiday.

Mandy felt bad for Gina because, at that rate, Gina would only have three more times to use the parasol before she turned eleven.

Thanksgiving came, and the entire family arrived at Gigi's house that morning. Grandma had visited three days before, helping Gigi prepare the home.

The kids all gathered around Danny because he was showing off the gnarly scar from his surgery. Even Mandy had to admit that it looked cool.

When Thanksgiving dinner time finally arrived, the older cousins—Gina, Mandy, Mickey, and Danny—found the old card table with the worn green top set up in the corner of the dining room. Grandma had made name tags for everyone and placed them on their plates, so they all knew where to sit. The younger cousins had chairs next to their parents, who would control the chaos of little kids at dinner.

While they were eating the delicious turkey dinner, complete with stuffing, mashed potatoes, and cranberry sauce, Mickey said, "Hey, look, it's snowing outside! I guess there won't be any parasol stories today."

Gina sat stock-still, watching the snow. Finally, she brought her hand up to her eye and brushed away a single tear. Then she stood, tucked in her chair, and bolted from the table and ran upstairs, sobbing.

Mandy felt many conflicting emotions all at once. But chief among them was an anxious twinge. *This fun won't last forever,* she thought. *I need to make a dragonstone quick—before my time runs out too.*

The next morning, everyone ate Grandma's famous cinnamon rolls for breakfast. There was also freshly squeezed orange juice, tall glasses of milk, and huge white china cups full of steaming black coffee. It was pretty quiet during breakfast—Grandma's cinnamon rolls were *that* good.

Outside, the sun shone brightly, glistening on the newly fallen snow. Mandy looked through the dining room window at the Circle of the Parasol and saw that the dads had shoveled it out—and already had a bonfire burning.

Blankets and winter attire were lying next to the back door. Two piles of birthday presents, one with superhero wrapping paper (*Must be Danny's presents,* Mandy thought, recalling his love for Spider-Man) and one with mostly pink-wrapped gifts (*Gina's,* Mandy thought), were stacked in the living room.

"Hurry up and eat, you guys!" whined Danny. "We need to use the parasol before the sun gets blocked by more clouds! Then me and Gina get to open presents!"

Mandy quickly bundled up with her favorite navy blue coat, the one with the big black buttons, tan knitted mittens, and, for good measure, a well-worn brown cotton blanket of indeterminate age (but known warming properties), and another cinnamon roll (they really were *that* good) and headed out to the fire pit with everyone else.

"I'm sure glad it's sunny," Gina said, as she sat down on a stump by the fire.

The older cousins grouped around her and discussed in what order they would use the parasol today. Gina said she wanted to go last. Danny was nervous about using it for the first time and wanted Mickey and Mandy to go before him. It was decided that Mickey would go first, then Mandy, followed by Danny, and finally, Gina.

"OK," Gigi said, "let's get this party started." She handed the parasol to Mickey.

"Thank you!" he chirped. He opened it and placed it on his shoulder.

With the parasol opened fully, Mandy could see the artwork that spread from its center, where the white dragonstone gleamed in the sun. Vines and leaves in shades of very light green were inlaid across the surface of the beige parasol. Each vine had dozens of small flower buds of different colors.

Mickey smiled at everyone and said, "OK! Here we go!" and started twirling the parasol. Instantly the dragonstone flashed a bright purple light, and Mickey was frozen still—with a big grin on his face.

After about ten minutes, during which time the parents, as they always did, checked their watches about a hundred times, Mickey popped back to life and said, "Neato!"

Everyone else applauded and clamored for his story.

Not one to easily cede being the center of attention, Mickey entertained everyone with a story of being a high-performance race car driver in a sort of "Olympics of Racing."

"It was amazing!" he said. "I got to be in several different races in one day. One event was drag racing. And I got to drive a big purple car with extra-large black rear tires, a tiny steering wheel, a jet engine—and a parachute to stop the car at the end of each race. Totally cool!

"Then I was also in an Indy-style race of one hundred laps around a huge red brick track. Then I did an off-road endurance race in a cool purple dune buggy with oversize tires with 'MICKEY' in white letters six inches high on each tire. I won two of three races with my buggy!" He rolled his eyes and continued, "I only lost once to a yellow dune buggy in the cool endurance race event. And you know what? That yellow dune buggy was driven by a girl I thought I knew. She was wearing a red and yellow jacket and a silver helmet with blue and green lightning symbols on it. She looked so... *familiar!*"

Everyone started talking at once, asking Mickey questions about his story.

Then Gina spoke up. "You know, this girl in yellow has shown up in a lot of our stories. I wonder who she is."

Mickey said, "Calm down, calm down, everyone, sheesh! I don't *know* who she is! But as I said, she sure looks familiar—like I should know her and..."

Gigi quickly interrupted, "Well, yes, that's a wonderful story, Mickey." She turned to Mandy. "Are you ready?"

CHAPTER 6

MANDY'S SECRET

WHEN MICKEY HANDED MANDY the parasol, she lightly patted her chest, feeling the silver cross pendant underneath her clothing.

She closed her eyes.

She made a wish.

She opened the parasol.

She twirled the parasol and...

With a flash of blue light, her vision blurred, and she found herself standing in a dark forest, dressed in faded brown shorts and a dark green shirt. In her hand, instead of the parasol, she held a bow made from a light brown yew branch and a dark brown leather quiver containing a slew of arrows of various lengths ending in a rainbow of feathers at the nock end.

As she slung the quiver onto her back, she saw J.T. standing next to a tree and said, "Hi, J.T.! Good to see you again. Where are we?"

J.T. bowed and said, "Good day, Miss Mandy. This realm is ruled by an evil baron. We are in a story about a band of rebels, intent on freeing this land from his terrible ways."

"Oh, like Robin Hood," she said. Then seeing J.T.'s puzzled expression, she added, "Never mind. You never heard of him. Are we going to be rebels in this tale?"

J.T. said, "Yes. We need to get to their camp. Follow me, Miss Mandy." He turned and indicated a somewhat ill-defined dirt trail through the dense green thickets. Pulling a dull gray machete-like tool from the waistband of his brown pants, he led the way.

After thirty minutes of sometimes severe going, with J.T. occasionally calling a halt to their march so he could hack some branches out of their way, they reached the camp. J.T. slowed his pace, sheathed his machete tool, and strolling into the clearing of the camp said, "Have no fear—it is only I, J.T."

He was greeted with various friendly comments: some rude, some mocking, some funny, but all welcoming. The rebels, some twenty or thirty men, stood around a tall, thin man in green pants, dark boots, and a rusty brown shirt talking about a festival which was currently going on in the village near the baron's castle.

"That's Charles of Grey, but everyone calls him Charlie," explained J.T., gesturing at the tall, thin man. "He's the rebel leader."

Charlie was saying, "So the baron has captured a huge mystical dragon. He's using it to scare the villagers. He wants them, and us, as his slaves. We are in it deep now!"

Mandy's heart leaped. *Finally! A dragon to make my dragonstone!* she thought with excitement. *But how will I get to be alone with it to do that?* She clutched at the chain hanging around her neck.

As Mandy listened, Charlie laid out a plan to sneak into the festival and free the dragon. The plan required the best archer of the group to use a metal-tipped arrow to break the locks on the chains holding the dragon. "But," said Charlie, "the closest anyone can get to the dragon will be well over one hundred yards away."

This announcement triggered much discussion among the assembled rebels: *Can it be done? Who will take the shot? There must be multiple locks—how do we deal with that?*

Finally, Charlie spoke in a loud, commanding voice, "Enough! We *will* do it! So that we choose the best archer, we must hold an archery contest. The winner will break the locks during our attack, and the rest of you will cause diversions. Come, let's go to the big clearing and get started—time is not on our side."

Aha, thought Mandy. *Now I see why I have a bow. But I've never shot an arrow before!*

Charlie led the group into a large open field of ankle-high yellow flowers that felt soft and cushioning beneath Mandy's feet. The area was ringed with tall brown oak trees, their leaves shining and reflecting the bright afternoon sun.

Charlie pointed to a lad with shiny black hair of sixteen or so years and said, "You, boy—fetch one of the archery targets we've been using and set up a target a hundred yards or so away."

Squinting in the bright sunlight, Mandy watched the other archers, noticing how they aimed their bows and how they notched arrows to the string. She wondered if she could even get near the target, but she trusted the magic of her bow.

It turned out her trust was not in vain. When it was her turn, all five arrows hit the target!

Charlie tallied the scores. "We will take the top five archers and draw straws for shooting order in a shootout. Each archer will get just one shot. Closest to the center of the bull's-eye will save the dragon."

He began to call out the names of the archers. Mandy's name was the last of the five.

J.T. said, "Congratulations, Miss Mandy!"

Mandy watched as a very short rebel dressed entirely in blue, gathered up five pieces of yellow straw, and arranged them in his hand, so they all appeared to be of the same height. He held his fist out to the five assembled archers. The chosen archers took turns pulling them from his hand.

Mandy drew the longest straw and said, "I'll shoot last!" Out of the corner of her eye, she saw J.T. nod.

The first two archers hit the target but missed the bull's-eye. The next rebel fired his arrow and hit the bull's-eye, almost dead center, drawing a roar of approval from everyone watching.

The fourth archer was so nervous his shot completely missed the target.

"Your turn, Miss Mandy," J.T. whispered in Mandy's ear.

As she took her position to shoot, she thought, *Close your eyes and picture what you need to do. Then open your eyes, fix on the target, and fire. The bow and the arrow will know what to do.*

Mandy closed her eyes, took a deep breath, and raised her bow. Not a sound except the birds in the trees. She opened her eyes, felt them lock on the target, and fired her arrow.

Dead center!

Mandy's ears rung with the cheers from the crowd as they went wild with the uncanny accuracy of her shot. They lifted her onto their shoulders. J.T. was laughing with joy. He walked behind the cheering crowd as they carried Mandy back to camp.

Sometime later, Mandy, J.T., and the rebels changed clothing to blend in with the peasants in the village. One by one, each rebel left camp and made their way by scores of trails, paths, roads, and other routes into the village and the festival.

When it was time for Mandy and J.T. to leave, J.T. said, "One moment, please, Miss Mandy. I need to cast a small spell. It will cause your parasol to transform into an ordinary-looking walking stick." When J.T. saw the look of concern creep into Mandy's face, he added, "Fear not, Miss Mandy. It will turn into a bow when you need it." He patted her on the shoulder.

Mandy and J.T. made their way via a dusty cart path split by soft green weeds. When they arrived at the village, they walked in through the imposing dark wood gates without incident and made their way around the festival. The aromas of a host of foods met their noses. The air was alive with the sounds of people enjoying the festival. Here and there, Mandy or J.T. took part in this or that activity, the better to blend in.

Eventually, they arrived at the far end of the village. Mandy spotted the dragon on the other side of a vast moat.

A stout, dark metal chain was fastened around the dragon's neck and attached to a black metal ring set into the stone wall of the castle. The great beast strained against a similarly impressive chain around each of his four legs. A smaller chain around his jaws kept him from freeing himself with his dragon breath. The dragon moved stiffly, impatiently, its eyes glowing green. The muted sounds coming from the dragon's closed mouth sounded like a mixture of fury, resentment, intention, and revenge.

"Look, J.T.!" Mandy said excitedly. "The dragon is *blue*. Is it possible this dragon is Vito, from Talon?"

"Yes, I believe it is," replied J.T. "It certainly looks like him. And since dragons are mystical, maybe they can travel from realm to realm in Storyworld. It may be that he ventured into this realm and got captured."

Mandy pulled her gaze from the dragon and looked around the scene. She saw a sudden movement; it was one of the rebels waving a small white-and-blue-checkered flag. *That's it!* Mandy thought. *That's the signal that the rebels are ready and in position to carry out their plan.*

J.T. saw the flag as well. He closed his eyes as if focusing all his energy. Then he looked straight up into the sky and gave out a cry that sounded just like a crow. This was the signal that Mandy was ready, as well. After a couple of moments, the white and blue flag began to bob straight up and down.

"The rebels heard you, J.T.!" Mandy said.

"Look, Miss Mandy," said J.T., pointing to where the white-and-blue-checkered flag had been. The flag had been replaced with a red-and-white-striped flag. This told Mandy and J.T. that the rebels had just started a fight with the baron's guards—the distraction everyone had agreed on. It was time for Mandy and J.T. to swing into action.

Looking at the staff in her hand, Mandy closed her eyes, calmed her mind, and said, "I need my bow."

J.T. watched as the staff moved and stretched and bent and changed into a bow and a quiver containing five arrows. Mandy opened her eyes, slung the quiver over her left shoulder, and pulled an arrow from it.

As she had done before, she quickly locked her eyes on the target and fired each arrow in rapid order.

The first three arrows streaked straight and true and struck the locks holding the dragon's front feet and the chain around the dragon's mouth. As soon as his jaws were free, the dragon looked at the chains holding his back feet, narrowed his green eyes to mere slits, and spat dragon fire onto the locks.

The dragon turned and fixed a fearful scowl on the chain that held it to the castle wall. His eyes narrowed again, and a bright arc of dragon fire melted that chain in two. The dragon was now free!

The dragon whipped its massive tail back and forth, crouched down, and let out a terrific echoing roar as it leaped across the castle's imposing moat. With a quick backward glance to Mandy and J.T., the dragon turned, ready to charge into the village to help the rebels.

"Hurry, Miss Mandy, let's get back to camp!" J.T. urged. He grabbed Mandy's right hand, and they began walking quickly toward the village. "No, wait," Mandy said as she veered away and hopped on the dragon's back. "Fly, Vito! Fly!" she commanded.

Vito turned his great head as if to attack some stranger who had dared mount the great beast. Mandy held her breath. But just then, the dragon stopped and bowed its head slightly—as if he knew Mandy! With a mighty flap of his wings, the dragon flew into the air with Mandy firmly seated on his neck.

Looking toward the ground, Mandy saw the red-suited soldiers of the baron regrouping to counterattack the rebels. "Down there," she pointed. "Vito, you need to put a wall of fire between the red suits and the rebels over there, so our friends the rebels can escape!"

Vito's great head bowed yet again. He turned in the air and sped down toward the soldiers, his vast wings flapping rhythmically. Mandy tucked herself as close to the great beast's neck as she could get, holding on tight and sliding her feet under its scales. The wind was fierce in Mandy's face as Vito flew just above tree-top height. With a roar, he spewed flames across the entire field between the baron's soldiers and the rebels. Mandy could feel the intense heat from his attack. She was thankful she wasn't down there!

Then Mandy felt the beast turn its head up toward the sky, and with just a few firm flaps of his wings, he soared high into the air and away toward the center of the forest. When she saw a clearing in the trees, Mandy directed the dragon to land there. Once on the ground, she hopped off the dragon's back and walked around to face him.

"Thank you for freeing me, Mandy the Witch," Vito said.

"I'm pleased that I could," Mandy said, then added, "I wonder if you could do something for me."

"Anything you wish, Mandy the Witch," Vito said as he bowed his head.

Mandy reached behind her neck and undid the clasp of her necklace. She held the cross in her hand. "Please, can you turn this into a dragonstone?"

The dragon looked surprised, but then his face softened, and he seemed to do his best actually to smile. Again, he nodded. Then Vito said, "Lay it on the ground, please. And then back away a few paces."

Mandy did as he instructed. She watched in amazement as the dragon lowered his head and opened his green eyes wide as if to take in every facet, every crack, every seam, every angle of the silver cross pendant. Then the great beast snapped his eyes shut. When he opened them again, they had changed to an icy blue color. The dragon then narrowed his eyes and began to blow a thin stream of blue flame onto the cross.

Mandy saw the cross begin to glow. It seemed to her eyes that every single individual atom of the cross was lighting up, one by one, with a blue glow not unlike the fire which the dragon blew. After about two minutes of this fire, the dragon slowly raised his head and without pausing, changed his fire stream into a much more intense deep purple flame. It was scorching, and Mandy backed up another couple of feet to escape the heat.

In front of Mandy's eyes, she watched as the cross changed into a more-or-less round glob, glowing like a bright blue Earthbound star.

With something that sounded to Mandy a bit like a cough, Vito stopped blowing flame and sank to the ground, exhausted and out of breath. He said, "Your dragonstone will be cool to touch in just a moment, Mandy the Witch. I hope you approve."

Mandy slowly inched up to the spot where the now pale blue orb the size of a large marble sat. She gently touched it and found it *had* already cooled and was warm, not hot, to the touch. She picked it up and held it tightly in her fist, absorbing its warmth before she put it lovingly into the front right pocket of her pants.

"Thank you, Vito," she said as she stroked his forehead. "Once you're rested, I think it is important that you should return to Talon immediately—you'll be safe there."

Vito stood up, shook his great body from one end to another, did his very best to smile at Mandy, and said, "Yes, Little One." The great beast backed up a couple of steps, bowed, and leaped into the air and began to fly away. Mandy watched until her eyes hurt from straining into the daylight.

Mandy found her way back to the rebel camp. When she entered the campsite, J.T. rushed to her and said, "Miss Mandy, the way you used the dragon to save the rebels was *brilliant*. But where have you been? You should have returned some time ago."

"Umm, well, we circled the village for a while—to make sure the soldiers didn't chase you," Mandy lied. "Then Vito dropped me off in a clearing in the forest, and I got a little lost before I finally found the path."

Before J.T. could ask anything else, the rest of the rebels swept Mandy away and pulled her to the center of the camp to celebrate their victory. A couple of rebels started playing instruments that looked like guitars, and everyone sang and danced.

Finally, after much eating and partying around the campfire, Mandy slipped into a tent, lay down on a pile of blankets, and... closed her eyes.

Mandy felt cold air against her face. She looked around. Her family was staring at her with eager eyes. "Well, are you going to tell us your story?" Mickey said and laughed.

"Of course I will, silly," she replied as she closed the parasol and handed it to Gigi. "It was so exciting; I just want to catch my breath first."

Mandy sat down on the stump and started describing her adventure. Suddenly she stopped when she was describing the rescue of the dragon.

"What happened?" cried her sister, Evie. "Did you get him free?"

Mandy turned her head, looking at everyone looking at her. She lowered her eyes. "I don't know. So... the soldiers started attacking me and J.T., and one of them must have thrown something. I think I got hit on the head and knocked out, so... my story ended, and I came back here."

"Wow!" said Mickey. "That's a first!"

"Yeah, too bad you didn't save the day," Gina said as she patted Mandy on the back. "But it was still a good story!"

Gigi stood up and said, "Let's take a break. I need to use the bathroom."

"Me first!" Danny cried as he ran to the house ahead of Gigi. "I need to go before I use the parasol next!"

Mandy's mom came up to her and said, "Are you hurt? Are you all right?"

"I'm OK, Mom," Mandy replied. "I was only knocked out in the story."

Mandy sat on the stump while everyone else got up to move around. Putting her hand into her pocket, she felt the coolness of the round dragonstone. Mandy never liked to lie. But she didn't want them to know about the dragonstone until she was *sure* she could create magic with it. She stared off into the distance, imagining what it would be like to have that kind of power!

CHAPTER 7

GRANDMA GOES TO STORYWORLD

T HE FAMILY GATHERED AGAIN around the fire pit, taking seats on the stumps. Danny sat between Gigi and his dad. He was so nervous and excited; he could barely sit still.

Mickey whispered to Gina, "I think he's going to pee his pants," and Gina laughed so loudly everyone turned to look at her. Gigi handed Danny the parasol and said, "Go ahead, dear. It will be wonderful! And don't forget to ask J.T. your question about the parasol that we talked about."

Danny opened the parasol, took a deep breath, and said, "Here we go!" He placed the parasol on his shoulder and twirled it. Everyone gasped as the dragonstone turned an inky black, and Danny froze solid.

After about ten minutes, the black stone turned back to its usual dull white, and Danny shouted, "Wow!" He handed the parasol to his dad and ran around the fire pit, clapping his hands and saying, "Yes, yes, yes!" over and over.

Finally, he walked back to his stump and asked if everyone wanted to hear his story. With a resounding "Yes!" from the entire family, he began to tell his tale.

"So, I was transported to the Old West! I had this cool cowboy outfit—all black with a sweet black hat and a pair of silver and gold six-shooters in these fancy black leather holsters with silver decorations. My horse was a black stallion, and I'm guessing it was probably the fastest horse in the west. I didn't see the parasol, but J.T. was there, and he told me it had transformed into the hat I was wearing.

"Anyway, I guess I was the sheriff of the town. So, a guy comes running out of the telegraph office, shouting at me. He'd gotten an urgent message that a gang of outlaws was chasing the stagecoach from the nearest town, heading our way. J.T., who was my deputy, and I jumped onto our horses and raced to head them off.

"Sure enough, after fifteen minutes of tough riding through the sagebrush, we spotted the stagecoach being chased by five men on horseback. We pulled our horses to a stop in a grove of tall oak trees. Sliding off my horse, who was breathing hard, I pulled both six-shooters out of my holsters, took careful aim, and began to shoot at the bad guys.

"Somehow, I shot the guns out of the hands of four of the bandits! And J.T. got the other one. Once they lost their guns, they all hightailed it away, with J.T. chasing them."

Seeing his audience was watching him with rapt attention, Danny continued. "I was going to chase them too, but the stagecoach driver had been shot and fell off the stagecoach, and I needed to do some first aid to save his life. And I did!

"Just then, J.T. hollered at me and was pointing at something. I turned and saw the team of horses was running out of control, straight for a deep ravine, *and taking the stagecoach with it!*

"I ran over, leaped on my horse, and raced off through the cloud of dust made by the out-of-control horses and the stagecoach. I wasn't sure I'd be able to stop them in time. I leaned down as close as I could get to the ear of my horse and said, 'This is it, big guy! I need whatever speed you've got *now!* We have to save that rig.'

"And my horse flattened his ears back, neighed loudly, and put on an extra burst of speed—and we caught up to the stagecoach! Just as we did, I dropped the reins, stood upon my saddle, and jumped onto the back of the stagecoach. Then I crawled up to the top, across the madly bucking carriage, down into the hard bench seat, grabbed the stage's reins, and hollered, 'WHOA!' The horses stopped just in time—and everyone was saved!"

"HURRAY!" shouted the family.

Danny said, "That's me, Danny the Kid and he, I, we... anyway, are a hero!"

Danny finished, "Just then, J.T. rode up with a bunch of men. Several of them were a posse from the other town the bad guys had harassed. Some were the bad guys themselves, each handcuffed and looking very nasty. We all escorted the stagecoach, and the bad guys, to my town.

"After putting their no good, bush-whacking butts in jail, the stagecoach passengers took me, J.T., and the posse from the other town into the Last Drive Saloon and bought us drinks..." He quickly shot a glance at his dad and said, "Just root beers, Dad!" Even Mandy had to chuckle over that.

Danny continued, "In the Last Drive, a guy was playing honky-tonk piano, and everyone was singing and dancing to celebrate, and I think I just ... fell asleep at a table in the saloon and came back here."

Gina said, "What a great story, Danny. Now, tell us about the parasol question you and Gigi came up with."

"Oh, yeah," he replied. "Well, before I fell asleep, J.T. and I were drinking our root beers, and I asked him if there was any way for Grandma to use the parasol even though she's not ten anymore."

Grandma sat up straight as an arrow and asked, "What did he say, Danny?"

Danny explained, "J.T. said that because you never used your magic, and never used the parasol, you *might* have enough inner magic to join one of us in a story. J.T. said no one had ever tried that before. He warned that there would need to be *enough* extra magic to boost the parasol past the one-person condition *and* handle two people going at the same time.

"You'd probably have to be touching the parasol, Grandma, or the kid twirling it, for it to work. That's what J.T. thought anyway. Oh, and he also said he wasn't quite sure *anyone* had enough magic to make that work."

After a few moments of silence, Gina stood up and stated, "Well, let's try! Grandma, will you go with me on what might be my last adventure into Storyworld?"

Grandma sat very still. Every eye was on her. Finally, after a long few moments, she straightened her heavy shawl, whipped a quick nod to Gina, and said, "Heck, yes! Yes, let's try this!"

The family started applauding, and even Grandma and Gina joined in. Mickey did not. He was looking quizzically at the parasol Danny's dad was holding. Mickey said, "Hey, wait a minute! Look at this! This was never here before."

He grabbed the parasol and pointed at a black flower bud hanging on one of the vines. "I know there was never a black flower on the parasol. And just above it is a blue one, and then purple, then red, and then yellow—all on this one branch of a vine. Danny, the stone turned black when you froze, and your clothes and your horse were all black. The stone turns purple when I use it, and things in my stories are always purple, too, which happens to be the color of my favorite football team. Mandy's color is blue, and Gina's is red, and—"

"Mine is yellow," interrupted Gigi.

Mandy said, "So, each of the flower buds must represent a unique person that used the parasol. The color of the bud matches the dragonstone color when they use it—NEAT!"

Mickey handed the parasol to Gina, then grabbed Grandma's hand and led her over to Gina. He said, "Have a great trip, Grandma." He kissed her on the cheek and walked over and sat on his stump to watch.

Gina sat on a stump next to Mandy. Grandma stood behind Gina and put her right hand on Gina's left shoulder, leaving room on the right shoulder for the parasol. Gina opened the parasol, placed it on her shoulder, and twirled it. The dragonstone atop the parasol showed short bursts of red...and nothing else happened.

Mandy thought for a moment and then said, "Grandma, put your hands *around* the dragonstone while Gina twirls the parasol. Let's try that!" They did, and the stone began to glow: first red, then yellow, then red and yellow, then yellow and red. The lights got brighter with each twirl, and still, nothing happened.

This might be my chance to try some magic, Mandy thought. *Am I really a witch? Can I risk trying with Gina and Grandma? What if something goes wrong?*

The temptation to try out her powers was just too great.

Slowly, Mandy put her right hand into her pocket and grasped her dragonstone. Very slowly, she inched her left hand toward Gina on the stump next to her. Finally, she touched Gina's elbow.

As Gina turned to Mandy, there was a brilliant flash of blue light, and the dragonstone on the parasol glowed a bright orange. Gina and Grandma froze in place!

At the same time, Mandy slumped over and fell off her stump. She felt dizzy after a tingling surge flooded her body. Her mother, looking concerned, helped her up to her feet and back onto the stump. Mandy said, "I'm okay—the flash of light startled me; that's all."

Mandy's mom reached into her large green bag and pulled out a bottle of spring water. "Here," she said. "Drink this." Mandy opened the water and took several sips. It felt fresh and clean, and she drank some more. She was remarkably thirsty.

A few minutes passed.

One moment it was quiet and peaceful, and the next, there was a big flash of orange, yellow, and red lights all at once. Gina came back to the real world and was showered with cries of "Gina!" "Welcome back!" "There she is!" "How was it, Gina?"

But Grandma was still frozen in place—with her hands touching the dragonstone.

Mandy drank more water and tried to look casual, although inside was panicking. *What have I done?* she wondered. *What if Grandma's stranded in the other world?*

Everyone stood and looked at Grandma. Suddenly, with a brief flash of bright yellow light, Grandma unfroze. She slumped and slid almost noiselessly into the white snow.

For a moment, everyone stopped moving, staring at Grandma in alarm.

Then Grandma's son, Tyler, quickly helped her back up and onto a stump. Out of reflex, Mandy gave Grandma the rest of her bottle of water, which Grandma drank from gratefully. Mandy stared intently at Grandma, thinking, *Is she okay? Does she seem normal?* Mandy held her breath.

Grandma said, "Oh, my! That was such a... a...rush!" Mandy let her breath out slowly. Hopefully, her magic had not done any harm.

As Grandma regained her composure, and everyone made sure she was all right, Gina closed the parasol. Handing it to Mandy, she said, very sternly, "We need to talk about this later," then sat down next to Grandma.

Huh? Mandy thought. *Did Gina see my dragonstone? How else would she know I'd done something?*

As the family settled down, they all anxiously waited to hear the whole story. Gina said, "Grandma, this is your first story; you can do the honors."

Grandma took another drink of water to clear her throat and began slowly.

"Well, let me see. The first thing was Gina and I became *mermaids*. And we were deep in the ocean! Just amazing! And something else, I became my ten-year-old self! I could not believe it."

"Whoa!" Mickey breathed.

Gina nodded as Grandma continued.

"And J.T. was there too! *As a merman!* He seemed amazed that *two* of us had entered Storyworld. Instead of legs, we all had fish tails. My tail was yellow, Gina's was red, and J.T.'s tail was a nice orange color. Gina and I were both holding onto the parasol, which had been transformed into a trident! It had a glowing orange dragonstone at the base of the handle, and—"

Evie interrupted, "What's a trident?"

Mickey replied, "It's like a spear but with three points instead of only one. Kind of like a large fork. Keep going, Grandma."

Grandma continued, "J.T. said that because multiple people came into the story at the same time, there was another important thing of which we needed to be aware. When you come into Storyworld alone and then somehow fall asleep, you automatically get sent back home. That's also true when multiple people come into Storyworld but with a twist. When two or more people come in at the same time, *all* must touch the parasol in whatever form it happens to be in the moment in order to stay in the story. As soon as anyone lets go, that person would be sent back to reality!"

Impatiently, Mickey said, "Fine, Grandma. Back to the story, please?"

Grandma started again, "Where was I? Oh, yes! So, the three of us swam together, and we saw dolphins, fish, and sea turtles. A pod of humpback whales swam toward us singing, and I could understand what they were saying! They asked if we wanted to visit the Lost City of Atlantis and that they could lead us there. Of course, we said yes and followed them.

"As we were swimming, Gina noticed a huge, great white shark swimming toward us, but it turned away and went after a baby whale. Somehow, Gina and I both knew the trident could stop the great white, and so we aimed the trident at the shark. An orange light beamed from the trident like a bolt of lightning! It hit the shark, sending it away. We swam past sunken ships and all manner of sea life before seeing a series of lights which the whales told us marked Atlantis.

"So, swimming towards the lights, we came to a deep gorge in the ocean floor. The whales told us that Atlantis was at the bottom of the gorge. The whales also said their work was done since we had arrived safe and sound at Atlantis. They sang 'Goodbye, keep following the lights!' Then they swam away.

"Sure enough, the deeper we went, the brighter and more varied the lights got. We saw more mermaids and mermen. And then we saw…"

Grandma stopped talking and looked at Gigi.

Gina spoke up, "We saw *you*, Gigi. Well, we saw that girl in yellow—the one who's been in lots of our stories. But she was… you. You were a yellow-tailed mermaid, and Grandma recognized you from pictures of when you were young."

"See!" Mickey shouted. "I *told* you the girl in yellow looked familiar!"

"Yep, that was Gigi," Gina said. "Grandma asked J.T. how you could be in our story too, Gigi. J.T. said if he answered, it would count as her parasol question. Grandma thought for a moment and said that he should answer. So J.T. explained the parasol has an endless number of stories and adventures. To make sure everyone gets a different experience when transported into the same Storyworld realm, stories can be altered for the next time. One way to accomplish this is by leaving a remnant or 'ghost' of a previous child visitor in the story.

"He also said we had been on the right track about colors, too, everyone gets a color, usually based on the favorite color of the child using the parasol. That's why the remnant of Gigi was in yellow. Red is my favorite color, so that's why my parasol stories put me in red clothes. And now I guess we know Gigi's favorite color!"

Gigi smiled. "I suspected that the girl you were seeing was me. Every time you told a story when you saw the little girl in yellow, I remembered that I'd experienced a similar story when I used the parasol so long ago. Your stories were slightly different than I remembered, so I wasn't sure. But now we know."

Grandma added, "J.T. also said your remnant wouldn't know us because the ten-year-old version of you wouldn't recognize us. He explained that many of the children seen in the stories were also remnants...*of our ancestors!* How cool is that? They are now characters in the story with whom we can interact."

Gina said, "At this point, we decided that having had an amazing adventure so far—meeting the whales, exploring Atlantis, and seeing the wonderful things in it—we decided we should go home. Grandma asked if I would let go of the trident first. In that way, she could have a bit more time as a mermaid, and considering she might only get one adventure, I said yes. That's why I came back before Grandma did."

"But wait," said Mickey. "The dragonstone turned orange while you were frozen, but you said your tail was yellow Grandma. That doesn't match up."

"Sure, it does," said Gina. "Grandma's favorite color is yellow, just like Gigi's. And when you mix yellow with my favorite color, red, what do you get? Orange. And look, now there is an orange flower bud on the vine, right next to Gigi's yellow one!"

Mickey interrupted, "But where did that *blue light flash* come from?"

Everyone else was congratulating Grandma, talking to each other, and no longer paying attention to Mickey—except for Gina. She stared hard at Mandy and raised her eyebrows. Mandy flushed and looked away. Mandy thought, *I'm not sure I'm ready to share my secret. But I must be a witch because my magic helped Grandma get her trip to Storyworld! I wonder what else my powers can do.*

Grandma gave Gina a big hug and thanked her for bringing her along. "I never thought I'd get to go on one of the parasol's adventures. It was even more amazing than I thought it would be."

The family stayed by the fire, talking about the stories they had heard until Danny triggered a cheer from all assembled by saying, "It's time for PRESENTS!"

He broke into a run, and everyone followed him into the house.

CHAPTER 8

LOGANNA

AND, OF COURSE, AS it turned out, Gina's last time to use the parasol was her ocean adventure with Grandma.

The next day, a massive blizzard began blowing what promised to be white-out conditions soon, so everyone decided to pack up and go home early to avoid the storm and the dangerous roads. Plus, the weather forecast predicted snow, sleet, and no sunshine for the next three days.

Mandy helped Gina carry her birthday presents to her parents' car. Gina quietly said, "Mandy, tell me, what was the source of the blue flash? It had to be triggered by something or someone. Blue is *your* color, you know!"

Mandy set the presents she was carrying into the trunk of the car, turned to Gina, and tightened the collar of her blue corduroy coat against the snow's chill.

She said, "I'll tell you the next time I see you. Happy birthday, Cuz." She grabbed Gina into a hug, then sprinted to her parents' car, leaving Gina looking frustrated and a little mad.

I need more time to figure things out, Mandy thought as she slipped into the back seat of the car, grateful for the warmth it offered.

That night, Mandy sat in her bed, watching the snowstorm through the frost-tinted window of her bedroom. In her hands was her new dragonstone. She liked the feeling of the smooth, cool surface. She wondered how to use the stone to tap all the magic she guessed, suspected, believed...*knew*... dwelled inside her.

Tearing her sight away from the snowy scene outside, she snuggled down a bit under the warm, white goose-down comforter. She thought about questions she could ask J.T. that might give her even a tiny bit of information on how to use the dragonstone. *But how will I ask him without giving away my secret?* she wondered. *He might try to stop me!* Finally, she lay down on her blue jacketed down pillow and fell asleep with the dragonstone clenched in her fist.

Mandy woke with a start.

She was no longer in her bedroom. She was outdoors, walking...somewhere... in a strange world she didn't recognize.

She looked at her hands and saw rough, scale-covered green hands holding a scepter with a green stone at its top. Mandy felt somewhat frightened, tired, and confused as she trudged along the bed of a shallow muddy stream. She stumbled on a large rock just under the blue-green surface of the stream and fell to her knees. She investigated the water... but the reflection was not hers. Instead, she saw the face of an old, green-skinned woman with scraggly green hair. She wanted to scream, but something seemed to tell her not to.

She ran up onto a cart path beside the stream and stopped to catch her breath. Then she heard herself say, loudly and in a voice not entirely her own, "I'm free! The blue magic set me free! But where am I?"

All through the day, Mandy plodded on until she saw a castle far away in the distance. She immediately recognized it as Phef's castle... with the dragons circling it.

She ran to the trees and again heard herself speak. "Curses! I sense him! He must be in that castle! Well, I'll get my revenge! If there are dragons here, there must be lizards..."

Mandy bolted upright in her bed.

She realized that she was at home in her bedroom. *It must have been a dream,* Mandy thought. She opened her hand and saw the dragonstone glowing with a dim blue light. It faded almost immediately.

Mandy threw the covers back and stepped onto the cold wood floor of her bedroom. *I need to hide this,* she thought. Her eyes searched the room. "There," she whispered. She walked to her dresser. Sitting in the middle of the dark polished wood top of the chest was her jewelry box. She grasped the box, checking its lock to make sure nothing would spill. Then she carefully turned it upside down, and there it was: the secret compartment built into the bottom. Mandy slid the chamber open and placed the dragonstone inside. She pushed the compartment door shut, set the box gingerly back onto the dresser, and scurried to her warm bed.

Mandy fell back to sleep in less than thirty seconds.

The next day, Mandy and her sister, Evie, spent the day outdoors, bundled up against the thirty-degree cold. They built snowmen and dug a snow fort out of the mound of snow a snowplow left on the edge of their yard. When their dad came out to clear the driveway, Mandy and Evie hid behind a tree until he was a perfect target with nowhere to run. Then they pelted him with snowballs until he yelled, "Uncle!" In an instant, the snowball fight was back on, but with all three hurling snowballs at each other.

Mandy had so much fun she nearly forgot about her dream the night before. But when she went to bed that night, she couldn't help but retrieve her dragonstone from its hiding place and ponder about being a witch. She was still holding the dragonstone when she fell asleep.

"At last!" she heard her not-really-her voice say. "A lizard."

She was standing on the edge of a dark forest with towering pine trees that scented the air. In front of her, standing over a low, round bush with small red fruits, was a lizard as big as a car. The lizard's skin had the pebbled look of a crocodile.

Suddenly the lizard belched a green fireball right at Mandy.

Mandy's hand reacted almost by instinct. She pointed the scepter at the fireball, and in three seconds, it simply faded away. Then her voice spoke again. Mandy heard herself saying words she couldn't understand, and then the lizard bowed, walked toward her, and knelt at her feet on its two front legs.

"Let's build an army!" Mandy's voice screamed, and she moved forward and mounted the lizard's back. The instant she had climbed onto the beast, it ran into the forest. They traveled a long way through the woods, navigating around the towering pines by the bright light of the full moon.

Finally, they reached the front of a cave in the face of a colossal mountain. The lizard barely slowed its pace as it ran right into it.

Inside the cave, Mandy's vision turned green, like she'd seen in night-vision scenes from a soldier's special goggles on TV. Despite the lack of any fire or other illumination sources, she could see clearly inside the cave.

Dismounting the lizard, Mandy began chanting rough, rasping sounds.

Hearing this, the lizard bowed its head to Mandy and walked to the back wall of the cave. It walked around and around in a tightening circle until finally coming to a stop. The lizard lowered its body very close to the dark soil of the cave. As Mandy continued her chant, she watched as the lizard laid egg after egg onto the soft sandy soil.

After just a few minutes, the lizard stood next to what looked like hundreds of eggs. Mandy stopped chanting. She raised the scepter toward the roof of the cave, and the whole space inside the cave began to glow with an eerie green light from the stone atop the scepter.

Then, before Mandy's eyes, the eggs started to hatch.

She heard her voice say, "Yes, come, my army! Rise and grow, and your queen, Loganna, will get her revenge!"

Suddenly Mandy woke up with her mom sitting next to her, shaking her.

"Mandy, wake up!" her mom said. "You must have been having a nightmare. Are you OK?"

"I think so," Mandy replied, blinking at the room's bright light. "Can I have a drink of water?"

"Sure, honey," she said. "I'll get it."

As soon as her mom left the room, Mandy looked for her dragonstone. She saw a faint glow under her bed that quickly faded.

I must have dropped it during the dream, she thought. Her mom reentered the room. "Thanks, Mom," she said after taking a drink of water. "I think I'll be OK now."

After her mom kissed her goodnight and left, Mandy again walked across the cold wood floor of her room and put the dragonstone back in its hiding place. *I wonder if I am dreaming or if this is happening in Storyworld,* she thought. *I sure hope it's just a dream. Otherwise, Phef and Storyworld might be in danger. And it will be all my fault!"*

CHAPTER 9

THE ATTACK

NONE OF THE KIDS were able to use the parasol the entire month of December. With school Christmas concerts, cloudy winter days, Christmas shopping, and the occasional snowstorm, there just wasn't time to go to Gigi's.

Mandy's family celebrated Christmas with her dad's side of the family. It was fun for Mandy to see her other grandparents and cousins for a change. As promised, in return for earning good grades, Mandy got a new cellphone. She spent every second using it to text her friends, but especially Gina, who had also gotten a cellphone on her birthday.

Gina was still a little bummed that her parasol adventures were over because she was eleven now, but she was anxious to have Mandy and the other cousins use it.

Just chatting about it with Gina made Mandy even more excited about the upcoming family get-together at Gigi's. She was texting Gina and Mickey during the drive there and noted how warm and sunny the day was, perfect for a trip to Storyworld.

When they arrived, Mandy saw that her uncles and cousins were busy shoveling snow from around the Circle of the Parasol. Someone had already started a fire in the pit, too. Everyone brought blankets or sleeping bags to use to stay warm. Mandy's mom brought thermoses filled with rich coffee and dark hot cocoa.

Gigi and Grandma came out of the house, all bundled up, and Mandy ran to thank them for her presents. As everyone gathered around the fire pit, Mandy reached into her pocket and double-checked that her dragonstone was safe and secure in case she needed to use it again. Because Grandma had been able to co-travel to Storyworld, now her mom, her aunts, and her uncle also wanted a turn.

Danny asked if he could go first and take his dad with him. Mandy said she would go last. She needed time to think about this. *I must boost the parasol's magic to make it work for two people,* she thought. *But how will that work when I'm the one holding the parasol, as well?*

Danny took his position on the big stump next to Mandy. Mandy gripped her dragonstone tightly in her right hand. Gigi handed the parasol to Danny, who opened it and placed it over his right shoulder. His dad stood behind him, just like Grandma had done with Gina, with his hands around the dragonstone on the parasol.

Danny began to twirl the parasol, and the dragonstone flashed black and then silver. Mandy hoped that between Danny and Uncle Tyler, they would have enough magical power to get the parasol to work because then she wouldn't have to use her dragonstone to give it a boost.

She looked at Danny and her uncle. Neither was frozen. The dragonstone didn't look like it was going to work for just these two. Sighing, Mandy leaned over a little and touched Danny's shoe. There was a sudden burst of blue light... and Danny and his dad were frozen in a trance. The dragonstone on top of the parasol glowed metallic silver.

Looking around, Mandy noticed that while everyone else was watching Danny and his dad closely, Gina was staring at her. Gina took her cellphone from the pocket of her black-and-white-checkered coat and started typing a text. Mandy felt her phone buzz as it received a message.

Before Mandy could retrieve her phone to check the message, both Danny and his dad came out of their trance. Mandy thought, *This is weird. Usually, even though the story experienced inside Storyworld feels like it takes hours, the person or persons holding the parasol are frozen for at least ten minutes or so. So, what happened here?*

Danny looked a little scared. Mandy asked, "That was quick; what happened?"

"I'm not sure," Danny said unsteadily.

His dad said, "Wow...that was a trip! Danny and I both became jungle boys, kind of like Tarzan. It was really cool at first. The parasol became the vines in the jungle! The valet— you guys call him J.T., right? Well, we met him... *in a tree, standing on a branch!* I asked him about the parasol, and the vines, and J.T. said, 'As long as you both swing on the vines and hold on, you will stay in the story.'

"Well, that sounded good to Danny, J.T., and me, so the three of us made up a game of tag...*with the monkeys that lived in the trees.* Yeah, it was so cool! We swung on the vines trying to catch the monkeys, going from one thick greenish-brown vine to another through the top of the rich green rain forest. It was a blast!"

Danny's dad stopped and frowned a little before continuing. "Then Danny noticed some smoke in the distance. He called it out to us, and we all stopped on the thick broad branch of a tall tree. I said, 'Hey, let's go check it out!'

"J.T. said, 'No, I don't think so. I sense danger. I've felt this danger before, but not for hundreds of years. I advise you gentlemen to let go of the vines and return home.'"

Danny's dad said, "So Danny and I agreed, we both let go... and here we are.

"Yep. Hey, I'll admit it. I was scared, I guess. Don't get me wrong; it was *totally* fun while it lasted!" His dad put his arm around Danny and said, "Come on, son. Let's get a blanket and sit by the fire and warm up."

Gina said, "Well, J.T. said that the job of the valet was to guide and protect the parasol users. But this is the first time he warned us of something that scared *him*! Did you see anything? I mean anything other than the smoke?"

Danny and his dad shook their heads.

Mickey piped up, "Well, let's think this through. Since we've never entered the same story before, it's pretty unlikely the danger J.T. sensed would be in one of our next stories too, right? Plus, if there is something wrong, all we must do is let go of the parasol, and we'll come right back! So, let's go, Mom. It's our turn!"

Mickey's mom sat very still; a look of concern spread across her usually happy face.

She said, "I'm not sure I want to go now. This magic stuff always did spook me out." She turned to her older sister and said, "Joy, why don't you go with him? You told me you wanted to try this."

Yes! Mandy thought. *If my mom goes with Mickey, I won't have to take her. Then there won't be a problem with me trying to twirl the parasol plus boost us with my dragonstone!* She said, "Go ahead, Mom. We can go together some other time."

"Are you sure?" her mom asked. When Mandy nodded, she turned to her nephew and said, "Okay, Mickey. I'm sure you're right, and there won't be any danger. It should be fun. Let's go!"

As Mandy's mom and Mickey readied themselves to go, Mandy casually made sure she was sitting next to Mickey when he started to twirl the parasol.

This time she didn't even wait for the dragonstone light to sputter.

The second Mickey began to twirl the parasol, she touched his foot while holding her dragonstone in her pocket. After a flash of blue light, the parasol's dragonstone turned brown and Mickey, and Mandy's mom were frozen in place.

Nodding her head as if to say everything was going according to plan, Mandy took out her cellphone and read the text message she'd received earlier. Sure enough, it was from Gina. It read: "I saw u touch Danny! How r u causing the blue lite?" Mandy smiled. *Wouldn't she like to know!*

Mandy spent a few minutes scrolling through other text messages. Then she looked up from her cellphone, and her eyes slipped over to the sight of Mickey and her mom.

Mandy said, "They've been frozen a little longer than normal..." But just then, Mickey popped out of the trance and fell forward. Mandy noticed he suddenly had a long vertical cut on his right leg that wasn't there before, and there was a new gash above his left eye—and both were bleeding!

Mickey's mom rushed to him, whipped off her blue cotton blanket, and used it to apply pressure to the cut on his leg in an attempt to stop the bleeding. At the same time, she shouted at Mickey's dad, "Don't just stand there! Get the first aid kit from the trunk of the car! Can't you see your son is bleeding?"

Mickey, between sobs, cried out, "The... Lizard Witch... turned... Aunt Joy to... STONE!!!!"

Everyone gasped, turned away from the sight of the bleeding, sobbing boy, and looked at Mandy's mom, who was still in a trance... with the parasol dangling from her hands.

Mandy sat on a stump.

A terrible chill ran through her body. *Oh, what is happening?* she wondered. *The witch from my dreams is real! Mickey is hurt! The combination of my powers and the dragonstone I had made for me have caused strange things to happen, and for all I know may do so again! And Mom is in who knows what kind of danger! And it's all my fault! What should I do? I wish J.T. were here to help me!*

Gigi and Grandma had decided to take the younger children into the house. This was just too much for young minds. In the meantime, the parents tended to Mickey. Danny, Gina, and Mandy stayed close enough to hear Mickey's story as he explained what happened.

"We were transported into an open field with big granite rocks and boulders. The parasol had turned into a long rope, with the dragonstone in the middle, and we were holding on to either end. There was fire all around the field, and smoke was burning our eyes. Then we heard J.T. yell, 'Take cover!'

"Because of the smoke from the fires, we couldn't see very clearly, but there was a giant boulder next to us, and we ran behind it. I hit my head on the rock, that's what caused this cut over my eye. J.T. quickly joined us and said, 'You two need to go back home right away! But I need to tell you something first.'

"Just as J.T. was about to tell us whatever was so important, Aunt Joy stood up to look around the rock to try to see what was coming at us. Just then, a bright green light, almost like a laser, hit her right in the forehead!

"She...she...she turned to stone, and the rope started turning to stone too until it got to the dragonstone, and it broke off. I couldn't believe it. I got so scared, and I was about to let go of the rope, but J.T. held my hands in place and gave me instructions. Then, over his shoulder, I saw what was coming. It was a giant lizard, shooting fireballs from its mouth! One of them hit the stone I was hiding behind, and it shattered. A piece flew off and hit me in the leg, and I let go of the rope... and came back here."

Patting her son on the head, looking relieved at the fact that his leg had stopped bleeding, Mickey's mother asked him what instructions J.T. had given him.

Mickey replied, "He said the 'Lizard Witch' had invaded Storyworld. He said, 'Send Mandy! As soon as possible! *And she must bring her dragonstone with her!*'"

CHAPTER 10

MANDY'S PLAN

"I KNEW IT!" SHOUTED GINA, pointing at Mandy. "I knew you were doing something you shouldn't!"

Mandy's dad rushed to her and sternly said, "Mandy, what is all this? What have you done?"

Mandy flushed. *Now I'm really in trouble,* she thought, fearing what everyone would think. Her mom was stuck in Storyworld in terrible danger, and it was all her fault. She took the dragonstone from her pocket and showed it to everyone.

With tears in her eyes and between sniffles, she explained, "Ever since we discovered the parasol, and I learned that I'm a type of witch, I spent time during each story trying to learn more about magic. I wanted to know how to use it. I learned that the key to using your magic is to have a dragonstone. It becomes bonded to you by providing a dragon with something made of a precious metal, which is important to you -- for example, close to your heart. The dragon turns the metal object into a dragonstone with his fire breath."

Everyone listened, looking amazed.

Finally, her dad spoke in disbelief, "And you did this?"

Mandy looked at him. "Yes, Papi. The last time I went into a story, I lied about getting knocked out. I did free the dragon. He made a dragonstone for me in return. But I was only trying to help when I used it! I hoped I could boost the parasol's magic, to override the one-person-at-a-time rule. Then more of us could enjoy the adventures. I had no idea something like this would happen!"

Mandy buried her face against her dad and began to cry. Mandy's dad looked at the other parents, then at his wife, frozen solid, and said, "Now what do we do?"

Mandy pulled away from her dad, wiped her eyes, and said, "Now I have to go into Storyworld like J.T. said I should, and find out how to save Mom."

"NO!" said her dad. "It's too dangerous! I'm not going to risk losing you, too."

Gina said, "It's the only way, Uncle Zach. Mandy has to go to Storyworld as J.T. said."

Danny shouted, "LOOK!" and pointed at the frozen figure of Mandy's mom. She had begun to turn to stone in this world now too—her feet and ankles were gray, like a statue's!

A dark pit of terror opened inside Mandy.

Oh, Mom! she thought. *What have I done to you? I will make it right again! I will save you! Somehow!*

"I'm going... to... get Mom!" she sobbed. "I have to!"

Mandy's dad nodded reluctantly and said, "OK. But you come back the minute you've talked to J.T.! The very minute, do you hear?"

Mandy nodded and reached up, kissed her dad on the cheek.

She ran to the frozen statue of her mom, ducked under the parasol dangling from her mother's hands, and positioned it on her shoulder. She bit her lip, closed her eyes, put her hand into her pocket, and grabbed her dragonstone. She twirled the parasol.

When she opened her eyes, she found herself in Talon, the center of all Storyworld. She was standing at the base of the mountain where Phef's castle stood.

J.T. stood next to her.

In her left hand, the parasol had transformed into a small staff, with a blue dragonstone at the top. In her right hand, where she had been clutching her dragonstone, she now held a wand. A magic wand! And her dragonstone was at the base of the wand, glowing bright blue.

"J.T., help me!" she said as her eyes filled with tears. "Something terrible is happening to my mom!"

"Indeed," said J.T. "Evil forces are loose in Storyworld. Look!"

Mandy wiped the tears from her eyes. She saw flying dragons circling the castle as if protecting it. Ahead, in the distance, were fires and smoke. She held her wand in front of her eyes and realized it acted like a telescope. She saw a wide river, and beyond it, she saw hundreds of giant green lizards, just like the one in her nightmares. In the middle of the lizard pack stood a colossal lizard with a green-skinned woman on its back. Dressed in green, she held a scepter with a glowing green stone.

Mandy asked, "Is that Loganna?"

J.T. replied, "How did you know her name, Miss Mandy?"

Mandy told J.T. about her nightmares. "I thought it was just a dream. I didn't know it really happened."

Before Mandy could ask him more, she saw through the telescopic effect of her wand that lizards were trying to cross the river. However, when they put more than their front feet into the water, they burst into flames, turned to steam, and vanished!

J.T. explained, "The lizards are made up mostly of fire, which is why they can spit fireballs. But this also means water is their weakness, and so they can't cross the river unaided.

"But," J.T. said ominously, "unfortunately, Loganna will be able to construct a bridge, and then they'll cross and attack the castle."

Mandy said, "But then the dragons can attack them, right?"

"Yes," replied J.T., "but lizard fireballs can kill dragons, so they won't attack the lizards unless they have no other choice. But this is all of a minor concern to me. First, we must save your mother!"

Mandy sighed deeply and said, "Can't Phef just fight Loganna and banish her again?"

J.T. replied, "My master is using all of his magic to keep Storyworld and Talon intact. He needs to remain in his sanctum. If he uses his magic to fight Loganna, Storyworld will cease to exist, and your mom will die. My master lifted the safeguards preventing your entry in Talon so that the parasol would bring you here."

"D-die?" Mandy stuttered, and for a moment she felt like she was going to be sick. *I want to go home!* she thought. *Stop that!* she then told herself sternly. *I made this mess, and now I must use my magic to make things right again and save Mom.*

Using the telescope view provided by her wand, Mandy could see her mom—or the ten-year-old version of her—frozen like a stone statue behind the lizard army. She stood next to a big shattered rock, just as Mickey had described.

"But what can I do?" Mandy wailed. "J.T., tell me what to do!"

J.T. said, "The magic from another dragonstone can bring your mother back to life. Then, if she drops the rope, she would safely return home."

Mandy said, "But she's starting to turn to stone in the real world, too!"

J.T. looked worried. "Then we have to move quickly. When you return home, you need to cover her and the parasol to prevent the sun from powering the parasol's dragonstone. That won't stop Loganna, but it will slow her down and will slow down your mother's transformation to stone. Now, we need a plan for when you return here tomorrow so you can fight Loganna and the lizards."

Mandy gaped at J.T. "What are you talking about? I can't fight that!" She pointed at the hundreds of lizards on the other side of the river. "And I'm sure I can't beat Loganna in a fight either! We would need an army..."

And then Mandy got an idea.

She asked, "Do you have a way to summon the dragons down to us?"

J.T. nodded.

Mandy said, "Then, hopefully, we have two more days before Mom turns completely to stone back home."

Mandy let go of the staff...

... and came out of her trance, in the real world. She glanced down and saw that her mom's calves were now stone as well. She grabbed a large brown blanket, tossed it over her mom's head, and covered the dragonstone, blocking the sun.

Everyone gathered around, asking what had happened and what she'd learned. Mandy told them the situation and then explained her plan.

Gina's mom said, "This sounds crazy. There's no way this can work! My sister, *your* mother, is turning to stone—but you want us to go home tonight and bring you crosses? Pendant crosses?"

Mandy said, "It's the only way! That witch has an army of fire-belching lizards. We need our own army to battle them."

Mickey asked, "But how can we all go to Storyworld at the same time?"

"I have an idea for that, too," Mandy said. "But more on that later. For now, you need to go home and get me the silver crosses Gigi gave all of us on our baptisms. I'll stay here with Mom. Maybe my dragonstone can slow down the process of her turning into stone."

Then she pulled her dad aside and gave him some more instructions.

Gina addressed her father. "Dad, I'll stay here with Mandy. You can bring me back my pendant. It's is the top left drawer in my dresser." Her father nodded. Mandy smiled and said, "Thanks, Gina."

Gigi and Grandma joined Mandy and Gina by the fire pit. The rest of the parents gathered up their children and hurried to their cars to go home. Mandy curled up into a sleeping bag next to her mom. She held her dragonstone against her mom's leg, just above the stone layer. *Please let this work*, she thought. *Please, please. My idea must work to save Mom!*

But... she honestly didn't know whether her plan would work or not. She was only a very young witch, with almost no practice in using her powers.

CHAPTER 11

BUILDING AN ARMY

IT WAS EARLY MORNING when Mandy woke to the sound of a car pulling into Gigi's driveway. She felt the chill of the December air and smelled the brisk scent of frost but was warm enough in her down-filled sleeping bag and blankets.

Grandma was sitting on a stump next to the blanketed figure of Mandy's mom. She and Gina had taken turns keeping a fire going all night to keep Mandy warm.

Gina came out of the house to greet the others arriving.

Mandy peeked under the blanket covering her mom and saw that both her legs were entirely stone now. She tried to figure out if they had enough time for her plan, knowing that she wouldn't be able to battle the lizards until tomorrow. Today, she had to build an army. Her heart skipped with anxiety.

Mickey and his mom walked toward her. Mickey handed her two small ziplock bags, each with a silver cross pendant inside. One bag was labeled MICKEY, the other was labeled LAINA, just as Mandy had instructed.

"Where's everyone else?" Mandy asked.

Mickey said, "Dad stayed home with my brother and sisters. He and Mom thought it would be best if they weren't here in case things go... bad. Mom told me the other families are going to do the same."

Danny and his dad arrived a few minutes later, and Danny handed Mandy two ziplock bags with their pendants in them. Danny's dad, Tyler, also brought coffee and donuts for everyone.

During the next hour, Gina's mom returned, and so did Mandy's dad and sister, Evie. Mandy asked her dad if he got the other things she had requested, and he said he had and carried a couple of boxes into the house.

Mandy said, "Well, it's time I go back then, I guess."

She hugged Gina.

She hugged Evie too—and felt her sister sneak something into her back pocket. Mandy gave her sister a knowing glance. She didn't take the item out of her pocket. There would be time later.

Walking to the stump, she snuck a hand into her back pocket and retrieved Evie's item. Mandy then pulled her blue dragonstone from her other pocket and took a deep, quivering breath. *I can do this!* she told herself. *I must do this!* She announced, "OK. I'm ready. Let's do this. Someone, please pull the blanket away."

Grandma carefully pulled the blanket off and said, "Good luck, dear. Be careful!"

Mandy somewhat clumsily started to twirl the parasol with the hand holding the ziplock bags. Her dragonstone was in her other hand.

With a brilliant flash of blue light, Mandy was transported to Talon.

She stood next to J.T., who had his hands raised and was chanting words in the strange language that Phef had used before—but this time, she understood what he was saying! She held her magic wand in her right hand, and the parasol, having transformed into a lean, tan staff, was in her left. The ziplock bags were propped next to her left tennis shoe at her feet. She retrieved the bags and juggled them into her right hand.

Ahead, she saw that Loganna had created a bridge across the river. Lizards crawled across in single file, but they seemed to collide with some sort of magical barrier once they got across. Mandy smiled. *Good!* she thought. *J.T. is using his magic to create a barrier to slow the lizards' progress.*

But now, she needed his help.

"J.T.," she said earnestly, "you need to summon Vito and some other dragons to take us away from here. And the rest of the dragons will have to keep Loganna away from the mountain and the castle while we are gone."

J.T. stopped chanting.

Looking skyward, he spoke some words, and immediately Vito, the blue dragon that had created Mandy's dragonstone, began to glide down to them. J.T. and Mandy scampered up onto his back, and as soon as they each had solid handholds on the great beast's blue scales, the dragon took off flying.

Once the rhythmic beats of the dragon's vast wings had carried them high enough, Mandy could see lizards advancing toward the mountain, belching fireballs as they crawled. She could also see Loganna atop her lizard, arms raised as she used her powers to keep her magical bridge in place for the lizards to cross. Seven other dragons soon joined Vito in the sky, and they all flew to the other side of the mountain.

J.T. leaned forward toward Vito's great ears and said, "There!" as he pointed to a small hilly island with dozens, maybe hundreds, of trees located in a sizeable mist-shrouded lake. Mandy thought, *Perfect! Even if the lizards were to overrun the countryside, they wouldn't be able to reach the island!*

Once the dragons had all made landfall, Mandy and J.T. dismounted from Vito. Mandy turned to J.T. and Vito and explained what she needed.

Next, she removed a silver cross pendant from the bag labeled GINA and placed it on the ground. Vito nodded to a brother dragon. He walked up to the pendant and began to breathe fire on it, turning it into a red dragonstone.

Mandy did this for each pendant she'd brought with her. Each time, Vito instructed another dragon to work, and each time a unique dragonstone was created. After the stones had cooled, Mandy placed each stone back into the ziplock bag from which it had come to ensure that it would go back to the right person.

Finally, Mandy put a silver cross pendant on the ground in front of Vito, and he created another blue dragonstone for her. This all took time, and through it all, Mandy kept hold of the staff to prevent going back to the real world.

As the dragons labored to make the new stones, Mandy asked, "J.T., what is that language that you and Phef use to create spells?"

"It is Dragonian," J.T. replied. "Do you understand it?"

"I didn't before," said Mandy, "but now I do. How come?"

J.T. told her that since she now wielded a dragonstone, she could understand Dragonian. Then, over the next several minutes, J.T. taught Mandy a few essential magic spells which he knew she could use when she battled Loganna and the lizards. He worked with Mandy until her Dragonian pronunciation was pitch-perfect, and she had mastered the art of channeling the spells through her dragonstone, and to aim them with the wand.

Once all the dragonstones were all created, J.T. helped Mandy back up on Vito, and the pair guided the dragon high above the island to scout the situation for the upcoming battle.

By now, most of the enemy lizards had crossed the bridge. They were using their fireballs to lay waste to the fields and trees in their path. They seemed to be waiting for Loganna to cross before attacking the mountain and Phef's castle.

Mandy told J.T., "I know how this will unfold. See you tomorrow!"

She let go of the staff and returned home.

As soon as she returned to the real world, Mandy shouted, "Quick, cover Mom with a blanket again." Gina and Grandma did, making sure they also covered the dragonstone.

Mickey rushed up to Mandy and said, "Wow, you were frozen for like twenty-five or thirty minutes! I'm so glad you're back safe, I was really starting to worry."

Mandy hugged him somewhat awkwardly; she still had the ziplock bags.

He continued, "But here's the bad news, your mom has turned to stone above her waist now. Did you get the dragonstones?"

Mandy said, "You bet I did!" and held up the ziplock bags. Dragonstones of many colors glowed brightly. One by one, she handed them to their rightful owner. Mickey's stone was purple, and his mom's was violet. Danny's stone was black, and his dad's was silver. Gina's stone was red, and her mom's was pink. Mandy held up the last bag. "Mom's dragonstone is yellow, just like her favorite color."

Mandy spent the rest of the day teaching everyone the magic spells J.T. had taught her.

One spell was to block the lizard fireballs. It could also block Loganna's green light. Another spell coordinated an attack. She also instructed everyone that the dragonstones wouldn't turn into wands in the real world—so everyone concentrated on getting the words of the spell pronounced correctly, using sticks as stand-in wands as they spoke.

They worked hard with only a few breaks: to eat lunch, for two brief rest periods, and then finally, past ten o'clock that night, when Gigi said they needed to stop for dinner and to get some sleep because, "Tomorrow you will need your strength."

Everyone eyed each other nervously at that pronouncement.

Gigi and Grandma had gotten pizza for everyone. They all sat around the fire pit to be near Mandy's mom, and ate in silence. Mandy didn't even notice the pizza's flavor. She ripped off chunks with her front teeth, chewed too fast, swallowed in big gulps.

"Slow down, Mandy," Gigi said.

Mandy nodded. "I'm just so scared," she whispered. "What if my plan doesn't work?" She stared in misery at the blanket-draped figure of her mother. *I want you back, Mom!* she thought.

Gigi rubbed her shoulders comfortingly. "We'll all be all right. We're all going to help you."

Gina got up and walked to the shrouded figure. She checked under the blanket and said, "Aunt Joy has turned to stone up to her armpits now. Her fingers are starting to turn too."

Mandy pushed away from the pizza box. "We will start the minute the sun rises tomorrow!" she said.

She crawled into her sleeping bag, next to her mom, holding her dragonstone against her mom's stone foot. Gina and Mickey followed suit, bundling up for the night and holding their dragonstones against their aunt. Everyone else with a dragonstone did the same.

Grandma put some more wood on the fire, helped Gigi cover the others with additional blankets, and then she and Gigi shuffled slowly to the house.

CHAPTER 12

THE BATTLE OF
STORYWORLD

A T DAWN, MANDY WOKE up as her dad gently shook her
shoulder. "Bebita, it's time," he said and pointed to a
large box on the ground next to her. Mandy got up and
gave her dad a huge hug as he kissed her forehead.

Everyone else stirred and started to stretch and wake up.

Mandy's dad said, "Grandma made her famous cinnamon
rolls for breakfast. Everyone should go to eat while I prepare
things here."

Mandy hurried inside and crammed a roll into her mouth.
She was too nervous to be hungry but thought she might need
all her strength for what lay ahead.

Everyone came out of the house and gathered around the blanket-covered figure of Mandy's mom. Mandy's dad was kneeling under the blanket. Then Mandy heard him say, "I'm good to go" as he crawled out from under it.

Mandy said, "OK, let's do this just like we discussed. Aunt Laina is going to stay here because we need to make sure that we still have a four-generation bloodline in place... in case none of us get back. Gigi, Grandma, and Aunt Laina are three generations, and us kids make it four.

"Now... when we enter Storyworld, we might immediately come under fire, so be prepared to use the shield spell to block anything coming your way. Get to cover as fast as you can. I have no idea what to expect, so be ready."

Everyone looked nervously at each other.

Mickey said, "Yeah, we remember all that—but *how in the heck are you going to get us all to Storyworld at once?* We can't all hold onto the parasol's dragonstone together!"

"I'm not," said Mandy. "My dad is!"

She pulled the blanket away from her mom and the parasol and said, "Since the parasol's dragonstone uses sunlight, we can connect them by light—actually by optics. As you know, Dad is an electrical engineer. He's been building an optical cable holder for the past two days. He's attached it to the parasol's dragonstone and then connected optical cables to that. He's going to attach a wire to each of our dragonstones, and the sunlight that will pass from the parasol will connect the stones!

"I think when our dragonstones become wands in Storyworld, they'll stay connected by light. Hopefully, we won't all have to hold onto the parasol at the same time to stay there."

"I sure hope this works," said Gina as Mandy's dad applied a clear glue to her dragonstone and connected one of the cables to it. He did the same to everyone else's as they watched, wide-eyed and in silence.

The battle ahead seemed like a weight that pressed on them all. Finally, Mandy's dad connected Mandy's dragonstone. She hugged him, whispering, "It will be okay."

But she didn't know if it would be okay, and her dad's face remained pale and strained. Mandy showed him the yellow dragonstone for her mom and said, "We will get her back—I promise!"

Mandy next hugged Evie and whispered, "Promise you won't use this until you have to, as we discussed." Mandy slipped something into Evie's hand and then walked to the parasol hanging from her mom's stony hands.

As she whispered, "We'll get you back, Mom," she noticed, with a horrible jolt of alarm, that her mom's arms were now wholly stone. Only her neck and head were still flesh. *Time is running out*, Mandy thought. *There might not be enough time left to save her!*

Mandy checked with everyone to confirm their dragonstones were connected and then said, "OK—here we go!"

She started to twirl the parasol. Grandma, Gigi, Aunt Laina, Mandy's dad, and Evie covered their eyes as the dragonstones each glowed as bright as the sun. Then, as Mandy had hoped, everyone holding a dragonstone was frozen in place.

Mandy was in Talon again. *Good! The same spot as yesterday*, she thought. And as before, she was holding the parasol, which had transformed into a staff, in her left hand. In her right hand was her magic wand with the blue dragonstone in the handle. A blue beam of light glowed between her wand's dragonstone and the dragonstone at the top of her staff.

On her right side were her cousins Gina, Mickey, and Danny. Each of them had a wand in their right hand, and each had a beam of light connecting their dragonstone to the staff—Gina with a red beam, Mickey with a purple beam, and Danny with an eerie black beam of light. On Mandy's left was her Aunt

Lilah, connected with a pink beam and, next to her, Uncle Tyler connected with a silver beam.

Mandy smiled; both were, of course, ten-year-old versions of themselves.

As Mandy turned back, she noticed J.T. standing several feet in front of her. His hands were raised, and his arms extended. He was chanting a spell in Dragonian. In front of J.T. was a massive barrier, like a wall. It glowed darkly. Above it was what looked to Mandy like a transparent shield of some kind.

As she watched, she saw fireballs arching out of the sky and headed right for the shield. When they hit the barrier, it held. But then the fireballs stopped, and a woman's voice cried out, "I sense the blue magic has returned. The same blue magic that freed me from my prison. Show yourself, witch!"

Then a powerful green light struck the barrier, knocking J.T. to the ground. The barrier vanished. Twenty feet ahead stood a giant, four-legged mottled green lizard. Its eyes flashed red and white, and its long pink and red tongue flicked in and out of its cavernous mouth.

On its back sat Loganna, the Lizard Witch, dressed in green and armed with her magic scepter with a glowing green stone on top. Behind Loganna were hundreds of lizards about the same size as full-grown tigers, waiting for her command.

Mandy helped J.T. to his feet and handed him the parasol/staff.

Loganna burst into laughter. "My goodness, what a frightening army of witches and wizards you have assembled to battle me. Pathetic! I assumed you were young, little blue witch, but I didn't expect you to be practically a baby!"

Mandy steeled her nerves. "We came to get my mother. You've turned her to stone. Let us pass so we can get her... and we will give you our thanks, let you and your army be, and return peacefully to our world."

Loganna burst into laughter again. "And let the descendants of Phef live to see another day? Live on to fight me? Never! You will all die today, and then I will take my revenge on that coward in the castle!"

"Enough of this!" said Uncle Tyler, raising his wand and shouting the attack spell Mandy had taught them. As he finished it, a bolt of silver light shot from his wand straight at Loganna. She raised her scepter, and the bolt was deflected past her, striking an unfortunate lizard behind her.

It exploded into pieces.

At that, Loganna shouted, "Attack!" and a great cloud of brown dust filled the air as the hordes of lizards, belching fireballs, rushed toward the family.

Everyone ran for cover, shouting the shield spell to block the fireballs. J.T., using the staff, launched a blue light attack on Loganna, rendering her momentarily immobile. He shouted to the others, "Pair up! Pair up! One focuses on blocking the fireballs. The other attacks! Don't let the lizards get close enough to bite or trample you! I'll keep Loganna occupied!"

His blue light snapped off, and Loganna roared.

And so, the battle was on.

Everyone on Mandy's side was doing their best with shield and attack spells. Mandy looked over and saw that Loganna seemed to be gaining the upper hand against J.T. She pivoted and aimed at Loganna, catching her by surprise. Mandy yelled to the others, "Change your attack every once in a while, to hit Loganna! If we mix up who's attacking her, she won't know where the shots are coming from!"

For a bit, that seemed to work, and Loganna and her lizard retreated some. But then Loganna shouted some commands, and the lizard army moved to outflank their opponents.

"There's too many of them," shouted Aunt Lilah. "They'll surround us and attack from all sides."

Just as a group of lizards surged from the left, a sheet of flame shot over them from above, burning them to ashes.

Mandy looked up and saw an enormous golden dragon silhouetted against the clouds of dust and the gray and blue sky, spraying flames at the lizard army. Mandy could make out a young girl in gold-colored clothes riding the dragon and steering it into the battle.

Then, as if in slow motion, Mandy saw a fireball headed right for the golden dragon.

And it merely bounced harmlessly off.

Mandy yelled to J.T., "I thought you said fireballs could kill dragons!"

J.T. answered, "I did. That is except for golden dragons, which are invulnerable. They are rare, indeed. There is only one golden dragon per generation. That one," he said, pointing to the beautiful dragon, "is Paction's daughter."

As J.T. spoke, the golden dragon swooped down to just above the surface of the blue lake. The great beast lowered its jaw, and Mandy saw that it was inhaling what must have been tons of water.

The golden dragon pivoted, flying up above the lizard army, where it seemed to Mandy it was perfectly still in flight. The beast narrowed its eyes as if aiming, opened its mouth, and blew a thick stream of water onto the lizards.

The lizards burst into flames and then erupted into steam, just like Mandy had witnessed when the lizards entered the river. The battle tide was turning as more lizards were destroyed by the combination of Mandy and her family and the golden dragon.

Mandy called out to Gina, "Focus on attacking Loganna with J.T.!" Soon, Aunt Lilah and Uncle Tyler were doing the same.

Mickey and Danny took defensive positions to protect the others, blocking fireballs and preventing lizards from attacking the group from behind.

Again, and again, the golden dragon returned to the blue lake for more water, returned to the battle, and attacked the lizard army.

Suddenly, Mandy saw a gap through their ranks. She ran toward the river and her mother. Two lizards jumped into her way, and her shouted spell destroyed them both in a red bolt of lightning. Without warning, a fireball came at her from her left, exploding at her feet and tossing her high into the air.

Instead of falling hard on the ground, she was grabbed by something that lifted her higher. She looked up and saw with some surprise that she had been caught by a winged lion, ridden by a young knight in shining armor with a golden R on his chest.

Focus, Mandy thought.

She pointed at her mother and shouted, "Take me to her!" The knight nodded and spurred the flying lion toward the stone figure.

As they approached, the lion dropped Mandy gently in front of her mother. Mandy immediately pulled the yellow dragonstone from her pocket and placed it against her mother's chest, over her heart.

For one endless moment, Mandy knelt beside her mother, holding her breath. *Come back to me, please!* her thoughts pleaded.

Behind Mandy, the battle raged with yells and crashes, and streaks of bursting light. When not exploding lizards with sprays of water, the golden dragon launched shimmering golden fireballs, which were so hot they felled many a target before actually touching it! The castle loomed in the distance, and the winged lion circled overhead, selecting its next target.

"Mom, come back!" Mandy begged, leaning over to breathe on her mother's stone cheeks. "I love you! Please come back to us!"

The stone face of her mother began to glow.

Then with a burst of yellow light, Mandy's mom fluttered her eyelids. Her lips twitched. More color flooded her cheeks, and her hands warmed as Mandy gripped them. Mandy stared deep into her mom's puzzled eyes when she opened them.

"Mom!" Mandy gasped, gulping on tears of joy. She laid her head on her mom's chest beside the yellow dragonstone and heard the steady beating of her mother's heart. Her mom's arms hugged her tight for a minute, and then she pulled away to look at her. "Mandy, what are you doing here? What is happening?"

Before Mandy could answer, they were both swooped into the air by the winged lion just as a fireball whizzed by.

Mandy said calmly, "It's OK. You can drop the rope now, Mom."

Her mother, with a surprised "Oh, yes!" let go of the rope she was still holding—and vanished into thin air.

She's returned to the real world, Mandy thought. *Right? That must be what this means.* Looking up at the knight, she called out, "Take me over so I can help the others."

The winged lion let Mandy down behind the remaining lizards and Loganna. Mandy shouted an attack spell she'd kept for herself alone and struck Loganna square in the back, knocking the green witch off her giant lizard.

Mickey joined in, attacking the witch's giant lizard. A short, fierce battle erupted, which ended when Mickey, with perfect timing, broke off the attack and stepped back several paces just as the golden dragon launched what must have been its 50th flood of water in this battle, this time aiming squarely at the giant lizard — exploding and steaming it into a large gray cloud of ash and steam.

Mandy's wizards and witches began to tighten a circle around Loganna, each shooting bolts of light at her while J.T. fired a continuous ray of powerful blue light.

Despite this combined might, Loganna would not yield.

Mickey shouted, "We have to hit her together! At the count of three...ONE, TWO, THREE!"

They attacked, forcing Loganna to her knees.

But in a flash of green light, she slowly, slowly rose back up. She let out a piercing scream, and a ball of green light surrounded her, growing larger and larger as it moved toward Mandy and her family.

J.T. shouted, "Don't let the green light hit you! Hit her again!" On the count of three, they again struck her with a mighty blow, but it didn't knock her down.

J.T. looked to his left, and a small smile appeared on his dirt-streaked face.

"Again!" he shouted. "Again, and again!"

Everyone in the circle attacked, but this time, a new beam of blue light from J.T.'s left joined the attack. With this, Loganna fell to the ground, dropping her scepter.

Everyone turned to look at where the new blue light came from, and there stood... Evie. Without missing a beat, J.T. chanted magic words that tied Loganna up and gagged her to prevent her from saying any more spells.

J.T. then shouted, "Miss Mandy, get her scepter!"

Mandy quickly picked up Loganna's scepter. Looking at it closely, Mandy saw strange engravings on it, and suddenly, a green bolt of energy shot out of the scepter and into the sky.

Mandy was so frightened she immediately dropped it and jumped away. She saw Loganna was watching her with wide, questioning eyes as J.T. picked up the scepter and placed it under his arm.

Gina ran up to Evie, saying, "What are you doing here?"

Evie replied, "Mandy made me a dragonstone. She said it was our secret and not to tell anyone because Dad thought I was too young to fight. Mandy told me that if Mom's neck turned to stone, I should attach a cable to my dragonstone like the rest of you did because you probably needed more help. Just as I was doing that, Mom came back to life, but it was too late, and I was transported here!

"I was scared and hid behind that rock over there. But when I saw you needed help, I joined in. Looks like we needed just a little more magic to beat her, huh?"

Mandy walked over, smiling, and gave her sister a fist bump. "For a little brat, you did a nice job, baby sis."

Evie laughed. So did Mandy.

There was a flash of brilliant white light, and Phef stood next to the captured Loganna. He smiled.

"My wonderful children," he said. "You have saved Storyworld, and you have saved me." Looking at Mandy, he said, "My dear one, you are a very clever witch."

Mandy smiled and then grew serious again. "What are you going to do with her?" Mandy asked, pointing at Loganna.

"I need to meditate on that problem. It seems my imprisoning her only made things worse. We'll have to see. I'll first have to think up some brave punishments." Just then, the winged lion and the golden dragon floated down from above and settled next to the wizard.

Phef said, "I sent these magical creatures to help you. It was the least I could do. Yes, each of them is one of your ancestors— remnants from when they were ten years old and used the parasol. First, is Izzy the Brave and her golden dragon, Thena. Next is Rocco the Lion-hearted and his winged lion, Marcos."

Rocco removed his helmet, revealing his curly black hair, and bowed. Mandy ran to him and said, "Rocco, thank you for saving me and my mom."

Then Mickey roared, "Houston, I think we've got a problem!"

"What is it?" asked Phef.

"Well, I figured we were done, and my leg was getting a little sore, so I thought if I just dropped the wand, I would return home. But I can't drop the wand. And nothing seems to disconnect the beam of light between the wand and the staff. And since math doesn't bore me like it does Mandy, I don't think I'll be able to fall asleep. Soooo... how are we going to get home, Mandy?"

Mandy shook her head. "I don't know. I guess I never tried to let go of the wand before, so I didn't know it wouldn't leave our hands. I'm sorry..."

Another major problem? It was all too much stress. Mandy's knees gave way, and she sat slowly on a large flat gray rock.

Aunt Lilah said, "It's all right, honey. I'm sure Phef will figure it out. You did so much and got us this far. You've done well."

Phef thought for a solid two minutes and then said, "I believe I have the solution."

He looked down at Loganna, who had pulled herself into a kneeling position. "Loganna," he said with a profound and deep breath, "it is time for us to move on. Our battles have gone on long enough, and so have our lives."

Loganna turned her head in defiance but stopped when she saw Mandy looking at her. Mandy thought that she saw Loganna's eyes shine, then change as if overcome with sadness.

Loganna looked at the wizard and bowed her head. Then she looked back at him, nodded, and closed her eyes in agreement. Phef took Loganna's scepter from J.T., turned to the others, and said, "For you to leave this world, so must I. I will take Loganna. We will continue to... the next world. When I leave Storyworld, Storyworld will end... and all of you will return home."

"And what will happen to the parasol?" asked Gina.

The old wizard, who suddenly looked quite old indeed, said, "It will become simply... a parasol, without any magic. Alas, you will have no Storyworld to escape to, but," he said with a mischievous smile, "you do have dragonstones, don't you?"

And with a wave of his staff, he and Loganna vanished in a brilliant burst of light that seemed to encompass, for a fraction of a second, each and every color in existence.

When the family next opened their eyes, they were all standing around the fire pit back home, holding their dragonstones.

Mandy rushed to where her stone mother had been...

The blanket was empty.

Wildly, Mandy looked around at the backyard. "Mom?" she shouted, and her voice echoed off the house. "MOM?"

EPILOGUE

"RIGHT HERE," SAID A voice, and Mandy swung around. Her mom had opened the kitchen door and was smiling at everyone. Mandy ran to her as fast as she could, flinging her arms around her.

Stroking Mandy's hair, her mom said, "I think I've missed out on a few stories. But all's well that ends well, right?"

"Right," Mandy gulped, her chest heaving. Together they walked back into the yard and over to the fire pit, where Mandy's dad threw his arms around both.

Evie squeezed into her dad's arms and said, "Don't forget me!"

Mandy looked at her parents. "I'm sorry for not telling you about my dreams about Loganna, and for keeping my secret about my dragonstone. None of this would have happened if I was just honest with you."

Her mom said, "Well, luckily, it turned out okay. We've all learned something these past few months, and I'm just glad we're all safe. And I'm so proud of you!"

At that, everyone joined in for a group hug.

Turning away from the group quickly, Mandy's dad said, "*Who's that?*"

They turned toward where he was pointing, and Danny shouted, "J.T.!" The children ran to hug him as Gigi asked, "J.T., how on earth did you get here?"

J.T. had a huge smile on his weary face as he said, "Hello, Miss Helen. It has been quite some time since I've seen you last."

He went on, "When Phef enchanted the parasol and created Storyworld, I was his squire and valet, and also... his apprentice. He took me to Storyworld with him. Since I'm human, when Storyworld ended, I came back to the real world."

He looked at Gigi's house and the cars in the driveway and said, "I see things have... changed quite a bit."

Gigi chuckled and said, "Well, we'll help you learn about that, but now that you are an official member of our family," at which point everyone nodded enthusiastically, "I think we have some witches and wizards that could use a teacher. Are you up for that?"

J.T.'s chest swelled so much Gigi was sure he'd pop a silver button from his immaculate tunic. "Indeed!" he answered.

Mandy picked up the parasol. The dragonstone on it had shattered, with a piece of it stuck to each fiber optic cable still attached to their respective dragonstones. Just a small chunk of dull white stone remained at the top. Mandy looked at the wires and said to her dad in a tiny voice, "I think we should disconnect the cables from our dragonstones."

Mandy's dad said nothing, just nodded and quickly freed everyone's dragonstone from the cables. Returning his attention to his daughter, he asked, "What do you want me to do with the pieces of the parasol's dragonstone?"

J.T. stepped forward and said, "By your leave, sir. If I may, let me keep those in a safe place. They may... come in handy someday."

With a thoughtful sigh, Mandy's dad gave the pieces to J.T., who slipped them into a breast pocket and buttoned it shut.

Mandy and Gina put their arms around each other and walked to the house. Gina looked at Mandy and said, "Mandy, *we ... are... witches!*"

"I know," Mandy said, "and now we can use magic in *our world!*" She skipped a few steps with happiness. "But first, I want to go home and spend some time doing normal stuff with my family. Especially...with Mom."

The End.

ABOUT THE AUTHOR

MARK EVEN RETIRED FROM IBM after nearly 40 years in 2017. *The Wonders of the Peculiar Parasol* is his first venture into writing fiction.

The story was inspired by his niece, Gina, who made up a game for children to pretend to travel to faraway lands and then tell the story of what they did and saw.

Mark is a long-time fan of comic books, superheroes, science fiction, and Harry Potter and tapped his enjoyment of these stories to create this story for his grandchildren's enjoyment.

Mark resides in Minnesota, where he enjoys movies, travel, fishing, birdwatching, golf, and, of course, his grandchildren.

Other books by Mr. Even include:

The Power of the Emerald Ring:
A Dragonstone Story - Book II

and the upcoming:

The New Lizard Queen:
A Dragonstone Story - Book III

The Destiny of the Lizardstone Scepter:
A Dragonstone Story - Book IV